A Pirate Flag
for Monterey

A Pirate Flag
for Monterey

The Story of the Sack of Monterey

By LESTER DEL REY

Illustrated by Donald E. Cooke

WINSTON
ADVENTURE
BOOKS

CECILE MATSCHAT, *Editor*
CARL CARMER, *Consulting Editor*

THE JOHN C. WINSTON COMPANY

Philadelphia • Toronto

To

Helen Knight

Under Many Flags

FLAGS are nothing new to Monterey. Spanish, Mexican, the Stars and Stripes—even one from the Argentine—once were raised over this California city.

The flag of Argentina, placed there by order of the pirate Hypolite Bouchard—who strove to defend his act by calling himself a patriot—came at the most critical period of Monterey's existence. This was the turning point in its road toward freedom. Several years previous, Mexico had tried unsuccessfully to free herself from Spain. Argentina had succeeded by winning the Battle of Chacabuco, and now in 1818 was trying to end all Spanish rule in America. This she hoped to do quickly through the privateers and pirates who formed a part of her navy.

At this time, Monterey—having successfully survived drought, famine, and the constant demands of Spain for taxes far beyond her due—was probably the richest of the Alta California settlements. It was the center of the forbidden smuggling trade in sea-otter skins, hides and bladders of tallow from near-by missions such as Soledad—Our Lady of Sorrows—and San Miguel. The half-starved Padres were compelled to choose between smuggling and abandoning their Indian converts, and the convicts and other disreputable persons sent there by their Government as punishment. Most of the good Fathers chose to trade with the New England ships that put in at Monterey. Many an eastern seaboard mansion was built with the tremendous profits acquired from these dangerous voyages around the Horn. And many a respectable California colonist and rancher made his fortune from secret rendezvous with these same Boston ships.

Knowing this, Bouchard and his men decided to strike a decisive blow for Argentina by sacking and burning Monterey. Loot in the form of gold, jewels, and plentiful food stores would mean not only riches for himself and his crew, but would replenish Argentina's none too lavish coffers.

This book is the true but almost unknown story of Bouchard's raid on Monterey.

Hypolite Bouchard and Peter Corney were real people. So were Governor de Sola, Comandante de la Guerra, José Estrada, Feliciano Soberanes, and Junipéro Serra. Padre Serra is only a priest who might have been. We have no record of him. Others, such as Jim-Jim, Hawkins, Montiféo Robles, Captain Obanion, and so forth, are also only people who might have been. They are fictitious, though many of the names used were actually present in California at the time. And even the people who are real are only as accurate as they can be made, since it is often necessary to build a man's character from a few bits, or to fill in gaps about his appearance, or the dates when these incidents took place. Much information is lacking. But it doesn't matter. Whether real or fictitious, people like these did exist then, in a land that was almost a heaven for a few years, before trouble fell so heavily on it.

Perhaps it was because of this brief war that California found foreign rule was no longer safe. Shortly afterwards, when Mexico succeeded in freeing herself from Spain, California also freed herself. In 1822, four years after Bouchard's sack of the city, California swore allegiance to the Republic of Mexico.

Today, as part of the State of California, Monterey is still one of the greatest landmarks of American history—and one of the most pleasant of cities to visit for those who love the accounts of the good old days.

CECILE MATSCHAT, *Editor*
CARL CARMER, *Consulting Editor*

CONTENTS

CHAPTER 1

Fire in the Hold!

THE wind was rising and the waves were growing rougher. The sails of the *Boston Belle* gave out a deep slapping sound as a sharp gust of wind filled them. The ship seemed to do a rough dancing step that rocked her masts from side to side. Then she settled down and began cutting through the Pacific toward California, leaving a boiling wake behind her.

1

The boy in the crow's nest atop the main-mast lowered his telescope and braced himself more firmly against the rolling of the ship. Miguel San Lucas Obanion y Boronda hardly looked strong enough to carry his name. He was tall for his age—sixteen in another month—but almost too slim. Only the confidence on his alert, pleasant face showed that the slimness was matched by a wiry toughness that was better than any amount of heavy muscle. He brushed the light hair out of his blue-gray eyes, lifted the telescope, and again began scanning the horizon.

From the deck, busy sounds reached him, and he looked down once more. Men stood beside the capstan, leaning against the iron bars stuck in it; they were waiting for the mate's orders to begin walking around it, winding it to lower the sails. His uncle, Captain Roger Obanion, stood studying the sails, figuring whether a strong wind was coming up that would make full sails dangerous.

Finally, the captain's voice lifted, showing just a hint of worry. "As she goes. And hold her east-east by sou'-east." He made a megaphone of his hands as soon as the orders had been re-

peated by the mate and helmsman and turned
his face up to his nephew. "Ahoy, Mike. What
sign of the pirates?"

"No sign of a sail, sir," Mike called down.
He swept the horizon to the west with his telescope again. Then, at a motion from his uncle,
he came sliding down to the deck, while another sailor climbed up to replace him. "It
looks as if we've outrun him."

"Don't you be counting on it," Captain Obanion warned. He was a firm, heavy man, with a warm Irish face, thin, red hair, and huge, but gentle hands. "When we had a light wind, we could show his heavy *Argentina* a clean pair of heels. But he has the advantage when it starts to blow. Maybe, though, since we've lost him and night is coming on, we can reach Monterey before him. At least, it's for that I'm hoping."

He turned into his cabin with Mike behind him. Captain Obanion dropped into a seat before his desk and reached for the ship's log. The page was open at the latest entry, dated for that day, November 13, 1818. Now he began adding details, the goose-quill pen leaving words behind as firm and strong as he was. But his face grew more worried as he wrote.

"If it was just the *Boston Belle,* now," he said, "I'd head a point north to fool him, and we'd be safe enough. But it's Monterey that's worrying me. Not knowing of Bouchard's coming—the poor fools are just sitting ducks for any freebooter with guns who comes along. Lad, we've got to get to Monterey before he does—we both know that; and that means I'm bound to head straight there—right along the course he'll be taking."

Monterey was Mike's home, and his own worries had been growing for hours. Monterey held his mother and his friends. He had been thinking of that far more than of the ship. "But Bouchard wouldn't hurt us, would he, Uncle Roger?" he suggested doubtfully. "You're flying the flag of the United States, and he's supposed to be part of the Argentine navy. Argentina isn't at war with the United States—just with Spain."

Captain Obanion sighed heavily. "No, lad, Argentina wouldn't sink a merchant ship of the United States—but Bouchard would. He was always a pirate, and no new flag will change that. Besides, he'll be knowing we may warn Monterey, and that he cannot permit. If he sinks us all without a trace, who's to know of it? He can go on and loot your Monterey in comfort then."

There was a knock on the door of the cabin, and a tall, lean-faced young man entered. Padre José Serra, distant relative of the priest who had first built missions in Upper California, was showing the same worry that the others felt. His ankle-length robe of dark wool seemed to hang on him unhappily, and his hands fumbled with the rosary that hung about his waist. He bowed his close-cropped head until the shaven circle on top showed baldly.

Captain Obanion shifted at once to Spanish that was nearly perfect, except for a faint Irish accent. *"Buenos días, Padre.* Our luck is holding up. The Argentinean pirate ships are out of sight."

"My prayers have been answered then," the young padre said, but the worry did not leave his face. "God has confounded the pirates as he must confound all who wrongfully try to rebel against the will of the rightful King of Spain. I heard your words, Captain. Pirate or not, what difference? The traitors who have mocked the King with their talk of freedom and founding an independent republic are not to be trusted."

Obanion lifted an eyebrow. "We Americans rebelled against an English King who didn't do right by us, and I think God was on our side. It seems to me, you trust us too. I have no use for Bouchard and his men, but why shouldn't Argentina throw off the heavy yoke of your King Philip's mistreatment? Why shouldn't every honest man or colony have freedom?"

"Because Spain is the mother of Argentina, as she is of Alta California and Mexico. Without the wise rule from the mother land, we would be nothing; we would have no law or peace, only savagery and chaos!"

"Sure, now!" Obanion spoke in English, then switched back to Spanish. "Wise rule, indeed! Your missions are taxed until you nearly starve. You're forbidden to trade with outsiders, and you padres have been forced to *smuggle* goods—against the law of your King, too—to such vessels as mine. Your colonists have been picked from the criminals of Mexico City, your soldiers are unpaid, and Spain cares nothing for you, except to take your riches and laugh at your troubles."

"A misunderstanding. When the King learns the facts . . ." Padre Serra began.

But Mike was no longer listening. It was an old argument he had heard often before. He knew they were talking only to try to forget the present troubles.

The long night and morning of fearing

seizure by Bouchard's two ships had left no time for sleeping, and he was too tired to listen to the argument. It was still several hours before mealtime, and his eyes were too heavy to keep open. He stood up quietly, with a questioning look at his uncle. When Captain Obanion nodded, Mike went out of the cabin to his own little one across the passage.

But when he was stretched out on his bunk, sleep would not come. Now that they were so near Monterey and his mother, he was excited, even without the pirates.

As a boy, he had never even heard of Monterey. Mike's life had been spent between Boston and Mexico City, so that he spoke English and Spanish with equal ease—as well as a little French the padres had taught him in school. Then, five years ago, when his Irish mother returned from a visit to her old Boston home aboard her brother's ship, the *Boston Belle,* Mike's Spanish father had announced that they were moving from Mexico City to Monterey on a mission for the Governor of Mexico. Captain Obanion had heard of the rich trade in sea-otter skins between Monterey and China. While they made ready, he worked his ship down South America, through the dangerous passage around the Horn, and picked them up at a Pacific port to carry them to their new home.

Monterey had become their real home almost at once, and they had no wish to return to Mexico. Even when Mike's father had been killed by a snake-crazed horse three years before, they had stayed on with his distant relatives, the Soberanes family.

Then Mike's uncle, Captain Obanion, had come back, suggesting Mike make the next trip with him. Padre José Serra had come along, partly to continue Mike's schooling, but mostly to carry papers from the Mission of San Miguel to the missionaries in Manila in the Philippine Islands.

It had been a good trip, and a fast one. The cargo of sea-otter skins and tallow packed in bladders had been exchanged for China silk and beautiful handmade objects of art. They had touched Manila, and stopped at Honolulu on the Sandwich Islands to restock with water and provisions. There the double blow had fallen.

Another Boston ship was just in from trading at Monterey, against the King's law, but necessary for the very life of the people there. Captain Obanion had visited it, and had come back with the news Mike's mother was ill—there were no details, but she seemed to be quite sick. That had ruined Mike's pleasure in the trip and had set Obanion to a feverish loading of stores to head for Monterey at once, at the fastest possible pace.

Then they had heard that two of the ships in the harbor were those of the pirate, Bouchard—the *Argentina* and the *Santa Rosa*. The colony of Argentina had rebelled against the Spanish King two years before, set up its own congress, and declared itself a free republic. It had beaten Spain at the Battle of Chacabuca a year before, and was now recruiting a navy to seize control of the sea from the mother country.

Among other ships, Bouchard's two had been given letters of marque which gave them the right to sail as privateers in the service of Argentina. They were notorious as pirates, and this new legal right to loot and ravage was made to measure for them. Bouchard was taking on provisions to sail for Monterey and seize that city and Santa Barbara, with all the riches the pirates believed they would find there.

Obanion had made it clear what that would mean. It would be no military campaign, but an orgy of murder and theft and destruction, with absolutely no mercy. Unprepared Monterey might be wiped out completely.

They had taken off from Honolulu with the double need of warning Monterey and getting Mike to his mother. They had crowded on all canvas and used every trick to gain speed, but it had not been enough. Yesterday, only about three days from Monterey, the lookout had spotted the sails of two ships that looked like Bouchard's. When Obanion had changed course, the pirate ships had followed.

Weather and Captain Obanion's skill had saved them once. But now would it all be undone?

Mike pictured his mother, sick and crying for him. Then he saw visions of pirates and savages chasing her out, burning the house, threatening her life with knife and gun . . .

He groaned, and gave up. He could not sleep. He had to get up on deck where he could watch the ship cutting the waves and try to force her on faster by sheer will power. Mike sat up and began dressing. It was nearly meal-time now, and he picked up dress clothes he had brought with him, since Captain Obanion insisted he wear them part of the time instead of the rough sailor's clothes. Mike was not to lose the feel and habit of clothes that suited a gentleman of Monterey. And Mike had to ad-mit that they looked better on him than sailor's clothes, even if they weren't as comfortable.

There was an open-necked shirt of China silk, softly yellow, with wide sleeves, that but-toned close at the wrist. Over that he drew pantaloons with a slit from knee to ankle at the side of each leg, and with a heavy sash of pure white silk around the waist. He slipped his feet into soft broadcloth shoes, and pulled on a short jacket of heavy blue silk. He was just reaching for a hat with a wide, flat brim and low, rounded crown when a sudden yell sounded from above, followed by a sudden rush of feet hitting the boards of the deck.

"All hands on deck!"

Could Bouchard have caught up with them so quickly?

Mike dropped the hat and jumped into the passageway, behind the figures of his uncle and the second mate, Hawkins. They swarmed up the steps and through the hatch onto the deck, where men were rushing about in wild action.

Mike noticed that the sun was now showing it was already late afternoon, but he could see no sign of a sail. Then his ears caught the ugliest of all words on shipboard.

"Fire! Fire in the afterhold!"

Captain Obanion rushed forward, and Mike could see where the men were clustered. Thick smoke was oozing up from the deck where the hatch was being attacked by men with axes. It was white and heavy-looking, with the acid smell of a fire burning with too little air.

"Hold!" Hawkins' voice rang harshly through the yells of the men.

Obanion echoed it. "Hold with the axes! Leave the hatch sealed until we get buckets going!"

But it was too late. The big ax in the hands of one sailor came down, knocking the whole corner off the battened-down hatch. Smoke rolled up in a choking cloud, and a tongue of fire burst forth, reaching for the air that was now entering freely. The smoke odors were a mixture of wood smells and the stench of burning silk.

Obanion's orders were beginning to bring some order out of the chaos. "Bo'sun, get men working on the bilge pumps—knock holes overside and into the hold below. Mr. Hawkins, get a bucket chain going. You—grab one of those buckets!"

The last was to a man who had suddenly turned to dive over the rail. Obanion's hand

wrenched the sailor back and tossed him twenty feet along the deck; Hawkins caught him with one hand, and shoved a full bucket at him with the other.

"Mr. Millard, get those sails down before the fire reaches them," Obanion ordered the first mate. "Cut one up and get sailmakers to sewing canvas buckets out of it. Mike . . .!"

He saw that Mike was already in one of the chains, passing the heavy buckets down the line. The strongest men stood by the rail, dipping the empties into the sea and hauling them up with ropes; the filled ones moved

from hand to hand until they were emptied into the hold and passed down another line. Hawkins was feeding two lines, and two other men each lifted for a single line.

Mike's arms were aching in a matter of minutes. In a few more minutes, they seemed to be coming out of their sockets. Then numbness crept in, and the process became automatic. His hands jerked as the buckets moved on, but he could hardly feel it. Still Hawkins went on lifting two out of the sea for each one Mike passed along!

After what seemed like hours, the second mate's voice snapped out sharply to them. "Full and empty lines exchange places!"

It helped some, but even the empties required too much movement of sore muscles. And the fire kept growing. It was now sizzling up too high for men to be near it, and the end men were forced to throw the water at it from a distance.

"Someone a-smoking where he ain't no business being, that's what must of done it," a voice beside Mike kept repeating. "Someone a-killing us all in our beds, that's what."

The bo'sun suddenly erupted out of the

forehold, reeling toward Captain Obanion, with his crew at his heels. Smoke was drifting off their clothing, and all looked nearer to death than any living man should.

"Spreading below, sir," he gasped. "Smoke's too thick—can't man the pumps."

"Tallow!" Obanion spat the word. "Those half-tied bladders that melted out when we were marooned. It's in the wood, makes it like tinder. Get some air, Bo'sun, then get another bucket line going."

Mike remembered the bladders that had been ruined in the hot days when they lay becalmed on the way to the Orient. Grease had seeped into the wood, and now was spreading the flames everywhere.

The buckets went on, but now the fire was too hot—most of the water was missing the burned-open hatch, and being wasted. Men couldn't get close enough.

Obanion stepped back last, his face bitter with loss and defeat, but his voice as calm as if issuing routine orders. "Prepare to abandon ship!"

The buckets stopped coming, and Mike looked up, surprised to see the padre two men down from him, with sweat running off his shaven head in streams. Obanion caught Padre Serra's arm and dragged him close to Mike.

"Mike, you and the padre go with Mr. Hawkins."

Mike's voice was a hoarse croak. "And you?"

"I go with the last boat," Captain Obanion said. "Get to your station!"

The flames leaped up, hiding his uncle's back as Mike followed Mr. Hawkins toward one of the frail little boats that were their only hope.

CHAPTER 2

Sail Ho!

HAWKINS, the second mate, was a man who never spoke unless he had to. His pushed-in nose might have been kicked in childhood by a mule, and his hair was completely gone, even his eyebrows. By contrast, his body was as nearly perfect as any man could have. Perhaps it was the shock of seeing head and body so completely opposite that had made people avoid him, and it had taught him to live almost entirely within his own mind.

19

At least he ran true to form now. With silent efficiency, he led his little crew of seven toward one of the longboats. Mike's eyes were blinded with smoke from attempting to find his uncle through the fire. Hawkins pointed at three other seamen and himself, and began undoing the ropes from cleats that held the longboat in position. Beyond, the crew under the first mate was having trouble. The rolling of the ship was ruining their attempt to let the boat directly down over the side into the sea, and first bow, then stern, seemed to catch and hang.

Hawkins waited, using his eyes to indicate which man should hurry or slow himself. Then, with a sudden shrug, he pulled the rope sharply. The longboat rose on its pulleys, seemingly without effort. It hung suspended in mid-air, and began to drop, just as the ship rolled low on that side. The ropes sang through the pulleys, and the boat was suddenly touching the water, sliding back against the side of the *Boston Belle*.

Hawkins threw down a rope ladder, and nodded the men over the side; he waited until the motion of the ship, boat, and ocean were right, then sent one man down at a time.

His hand fell on Mike's shoulder. Mike started forward, but hesitated. For a second, the flames had stopped billowing, and he tried to catch one last glimpse of his uncle.

One of Hawkins' hands caught his shoulder, and he found himself over the side, his hands near the ladder. He caught it and dropped quickly, just before a wave slapped the long-boat upward smartly. A second more and it might have pitched him into the increasingly rough sea.

Hawkins came last, half-carrying Padre Serra. "Cast off!"

"My uncle!" Mike gasped hoarsely.

A sudden smile twisted Hawkins' face—the first Mike had seen. His voice was almost understanding. "He knows the sea and his ship. He'll make number four boat." Then he was normal again. "Cast off!"

The sea seemed to be growing wilder by the minute, and there were heavy clouds gathering to the north. The two sailors holding lines to the ship shivered as thunder sounded, but they dropped the ropes. Hawkins, at the rudder, shoved the boat away. The first boat was already bobbing ahead of them, headed toward the distant coast of California. Hawkins steered after it, while four men manned the big oars, timing themselves by his count. They began to draw away.

The pitching of the boat made it hard to see the one ahead, and it was even impossible to see the burning *Boston Belle* when their boat was in a trough of the waves. One of the oarsmen missed his count, and the bow hit into a wave, shipping water into the boat. Hawkins made no comment, and the even count went on again.

Mike located the bailing bucket, but there was too little water to bail yet. Hawkins nodded slightly, and motioned the boy forward. From that position, Mike could see the burning ship better.

The third boat had been cast off and was following, but there was no sign of the fourth. The *Boston Belle* was a complete loss now, with fire running up her masts and out on the yardarms. Most of the deck had been burned away, including the section where Mike seemed to remember the fourth boat had been stored.

Then rain began whipping down, stinging their eyes, and the wind which suddenly took on an edge began wailing in their ears. The gloom darkened, until it was almost like night. Only the light of the flames showed behind to mark the *Boston Belle*.

Hawkins looked at Mike and nodded, somehow indicating that he still was sure Captain Obanion had gotten away. Mike didn't believe it. Padre Serra reached for the boy's arm, but

Mike drew it away quickly and began bailing the little water that had been shipped.

The waves were being whipped up, showing whitecaps on their crests, and they seemed to yell as the boat plowed into them, a wild threat without mercy.

But Mike had no emotions left. He went on bailing, while the storm lashed at the men and the boat. The bailing was no longer useless. The boat was shipping water fast, and the rain was a torrent, until he could no longer see Hawkins at the other end through its fury.

Two of the sailors were seasick from the crazy bouncing of the boat. Mike wondered why he wasn't, and then decided that he was too tired. But he went on bailing, and Serra came forward, on hands and knees, to fight the gale. Together, they seemed able to keep the water about level.

"Mike!" Hawkins' voice cut through his numbness, and he went back, crawling over one of the oarsmen who seemed to have passed out. When he reached the end, Hawkins handed him the tiller, and moved forward. A minute later, the second mate was seated at the oars, the unconscious man held up between his knees.

The boat seemed to go crazy for a few minutes, until Mike caught the hang of it. Once a splinter came off in his hand, but he pried it out with his teeth and spat it overboard.

At rare moments, the wind and waves would find a second of silence. Mike heard the labored breathing of Padre Serra and noted idly that the priest was timing his motions to a monotonous chant. "Pa-ter nos-ter, *qui* est in coe-lo, *sanc*-ti-fi-ca-tur *no*-men tu-um; ad-*ven*-i-at reg-num tu-um, si-cut in *coe*-lo, et in ter-*ra* . . ." Mike's own lips took up the Pater Noster. A few minutes later, in another lull, he heard his lips saying, ". . . Little lamb, its fleece was white as snow." He had no idea when he had changed.

The first unconscious man recovered, and took over the tiller, while Mike started to take the oars of another who was too tired to continue. Hawkins caught his shoulder and pointed to the water; Mike began bailing again, leaving only three men at the oars.

Twice during the long night, Mike decided they could not live another hour. Once he passed out, to come to between Hawkins' knees, his head held out of the water. He crawled around until he found the bail and went on scooping out water. This time the level of the water started receding, and he realized that the storm was dying out. Serra had somehow held on through the whole night, as had Hawkins. None of the others could say as much.

An hour later, gray light showed it was dawn. The sea was still heaving, but it was a steady, montonous heave now that could be met by steersman and rowers. The wind had died almost completely, but the clouds were still a blanket over the sky, though they let a vague, diffused light through.

Shortly after that, they could see the sea about them. From horizon to horizon, there was no sign of another boat. Hawkins was looking at the sky, trying to locate the sun, but it was hopeless. They could not possibly know which way they were going, or how far they had traveled during the night.

"But you have a compass?" Padre Serra asked. Mike translated, and Hawkins shrugged.

"Overboard—with most of our provisions and one cask of water." The mate was already pulling out the few undamaged things that remained. He indicated one water cask and a single tin of ship's biscuits. Without comment, he doled out a can of water and three biscuits to each man. Watching his eyes, the men accepted their shares in silence also.

They drew splinters of wood to see who should sleep, and Mike was lucky. He curled up in his soggy, soiled clothes on the bottom of the boat and didn't awaken until a violent tugging at his elbow told him it was his turn to row. He looked up at Hawkins, and was almost surprised when the mate also took his turn sleeping. But it was good sense; not resting might have endangered them later at some time when nobody could sleep.

In the afternoon, after monotonous and exhausting hours of spelling at the oars, bailing and patiently scanning the horizon, Mike had another chance to sleep, and when he woke up he felt somewhat refreshed. Now, after the drugged fatigue had lessened, he was more conscious of his blistered, bleeding hands, and the sting of salt in them. But the picture of his mother, sick and crying for him, was stronger than pain. Somehow, he felt he had failed her. He should have done something—he couldn't tell what—to have been with her sooner. He had no business going off in the first place! Her large blue eyes seemed to stare at him, accusing and forgiving, but the Irish laughter was missing from her lips.

"The missions—the colonists!" Serra, who had been sleeping, came to his feet, crying it. "They must be warned. Bouchard is coming to murder them. We must hurry . . . hurry . . . hurry . . .!"

"*Pronto,*" Hawkins agreed. He seemed to have guessed the padre's words, and used one of his half-dozen Spanish words to answer it. But the padre knew as well as the rest that they could not do it soon—or perhaps ever. They were lost, with almost no provisions, and Monterey seemed farther away now than it ever had.

But *they* had to warn the city—or it would be lost!

Night fell again. One of the seamen took up a low wailing cry as the darkness fell, and another picked it up hysterically. Hawkins lifted the first man in his arms, thrust him headfirst into the sea, and put him back on his seat again, methodically. The man sat numbed for a second, before trying to smile and slip away from the mate. The other seaman shut up abruptly.

"Pronto," Hawkins told Mike this time, but it was a warning instead of a promise. Soon this would grow worse, and the men might start going crazy.

The night seemed longer than any other—perhaps because the numbness was missing, and Mike was fully conscious of the time. Hawkins rotated the crew at rowing, but stopped Mike the second time, after looking at the boy's hands. The blisters were bleeding again, and the mate shook his head. He motioned Mike back to the somewhat easier tiller, and took the turn himself.

Mike wanted to protest, but he couldn't— the pain had been too intense. Anyhow, he knew the mate was right; if he got an infection, he'd be of less use than none.

Toward the end of the night, a few stray patches appeared in the clouds, and they saw an occasional star. But there was no way to tell which stars they were, since they could not spot enough to recognize familiar groups. Then the first light of dawn came. The sky was clearer now, but the light was too bright for the stars to show, and the sun had not yet come up.

Hawkins stripped and went overboard, splashing around. At his gesture, Mike and three others did the same. The salt water stung in Mike's sores, but it was refreshing to his aching body and he felt better when he climbed back.

Suddenly the horizon began to glow, and Mike pointed. Hawkins followed his gesture. "East!"

They had been rowing north—unless they had been making a circle! Certainly they had not been heading toward California and Monterey.

Now that they were heading east properly, there was no way to know where they might land. The storm must have carried them south, but they had been rowing north last. They could not even know when they reached the coast whether to head north or south to locate the Bay of Monterey!

Hawkins handed out only one biscuit apiece and half a can of water this time. The cask sounded nearly empty, and the biscuit tin must be in a similar state. Three of the men grumbled, but none seemed to dare to argue strongly about it with Hawkins.

Mike swallowed his scant rations, surprised to find that hunger and thirst were bothering him more than his bleeding hands. He inspected his sores, and was pleased to see that they seemed to be healing nicely. Maybe the salt water that had stung so sharply was good medicine.

"How long?" he asked at last. "I mean, how long before we can begin to look for the coast?"

"Five days to two weeks," Hawkins answered. He picked up the oars and began rowing, counting strokes again. Mike moved to the bow of the boat, where he could fall asleep again.

Then he stopped, staring back. A small swell was moving in the ocean, and he waited until it came again before raising on tiptoe.

"Sail ho!" The words came out of his mouth like the crack of a howitzer.

The others were up instantly, yelling and trying to see. Then they saw it. Just on the horizon to the south and west, the tip of a sail showed. The sailor at the tiller sat down abruptly, swinging the rudder, and headed toward it. Hawkins nodded.

The mate reached for two of the oars and began fastening them together, using his belt to hold them. His eyes swept over the crew, and came to rest on Mike. "White's best—see farther."

With trembling fingers, Mike unfastened the grimy sash that had once been sparkling white and handed it over. Hawkins split one end of the heavy silk with his fingers and knotted it to the end of the improvised pole. He lifted the contraption and began waving it back and forth, first rapidly, then slowly, then rapidly again.

The tip of the sail was clearer now, heading silently eastward, on a course that would keep it miles from the boat.

The men were eying Padre Serra now, and
the priest knelt, beginning to pray. The American sailors could not understand the words,
but their moving lips showed that they were
echoing the thoughts.

"Going past," Mike moaned.

Hawkins lifted himself a bit higher. "Tack-
ing," he announced.

Later, they saw it was true. The sail was
growing bigger. The light wind was blowing
dead from the north, and the ship was forced
to tack toward them slowly.

The sudden cry of a sailor swung them
about, and they followed his pointing finger
to the north, where another sail was bearing
down on them, heading toward the other. Now
that they saw both, it was easy to tell that
neither was heading for the longboat; instead,
they were moving to come together, some distance east of the boat, and farther to the south,
the second ship, favored by the wind, was
covering most of the distance that separated
the two.

Hawkins dropped the crude flag, but Serra
sprang to catch it. He climbed onto a seat and
continued waving the distress signal. Then

two sailors lifted the padre on their shoulders, supporting him against the swaying of the boat.

The second ship was closer now, heading past them to the east. A groan went up among the men—and was cut off as the ship came about and headed toward the longboat!

It was a good-sized, three-masted ship, with the solid motion of a heavily built and rugged vessel.

Hawkins looked at the men, shrugged, and dropped over the side of the boat. His head bobbed up from the surface, and he called to Mike, motioning toward the ship. For a second, Mike's admiration for the ability the mate had shown almost made him follow the man's example.

Then the boy shook his head. The mate was swimming with strong strokes, directly away from the ship! Now Hawkins raised a hand, beckoning. Between the frantic rowing of the oarsmen and his lusty swimming, he was disappearing rapidly.

Suddenly a chill ran up Mike's spine as he guessed the mate's reasons for his act, and he swung about to stare at the large ship from which a boat was being lowered. But Padre Serra had already spotted the name of the ship.

"The *Argentina!* Bouchard—the pirate!"

Mike looked back at the spot where Hawkins had vanished and cursed himself for being a fool. Two ships, one three-masted and one two-masted, so near Monterey. It had to be Bouchard! He should have known it at once, as Hawkins had.

But it was too late to jump now, even if drowning might be better than being captured. They were practically under the bow of the pirate ship, and the rescue boat was within grappling distance.

They were already captured!

CHAPTER 3

The Patriotic Pirates

UTTER confusion hit the men. Serra and a few of the others were trying to back-track away from the pirates, with oars flailing at the water. Two of the sailors were reaching out for the shorter pirate boat. Two others simply sat frozen, yelling with meaning-less excitement.

Mike stared after the vanished Hawkins, hating his own slowness in understanding. Yet what good would drowning do?

The leader of the pirate boat crew was a stout Sandwich Islander, with a face marked by the long scar of a knife wound, and the rest were a mixture of all races found in the Pacific. The big Islander was grinning as he stared at Padre Serra. *"Aloha, wahini,"* he boomed, and began laughing coarsely at his own joke. Mike knew he was calling the padre a woman because of the robe the priest wore, but he refused to give the pirate the satisfaction of showing his understanding.

The leader looked at the dirty, storm-battered longboat of the *Boston Belle,* held his nose insultingly, and drew a knife. His heavy body shook the longboat as he jumped in.

"Out!" he ordered. Mike hesitated, and the sharp point of the knife bit into his ribs, bringing a scream to his lips before he could stop it. He looked at the pirate with sudden, violent hatred, but the man only grinned and gestured menacingly with the knife. The other men were already in the pirate boat. Reluctantly, Mike climbed over, and the pirate kicked the longboat away. He called out sharply, and the pirate boat swung back to the ship.

"What now?" Mike asked between his teeth.

He was scared—afraid enough to make his teeth chatter—and he knew the pirates knew it, but he couldn't help it.

Serra shook his head sorrowfully, and his own eyes were afraid, which somehow made Mike feel less so. "God knows, my son. We can only wait."

There wasn't much waiting. They were jostled up the rope ladder onto the *Argentina* with the point of the knife constantly jabbing them on. A dark-haired man of medium height with the eyes of a wolf came forward, laughing as the knife brought pained grunts.

His English had a thick quality unlike the usual French accent, but this was obviously the notorious Hypolite Bouchard, scum and scavenger pirate of the Pacific.

"A scurvy lot of sea-pigs! You—where's the *Boston Belle?*"

The sailor he addressed jerked back and his eyes dropped. "Burned up, sir. And there was a storm . . ."

"Ptttt! The storm I know. Did it not separate the *Santa Rosa* and the *Argentina* until now? So your captain would warn the Dons, eh? Ha! We serve the new republic—for God and Country! And God throws you traitors to liberty in my direction! Ha! What do we do with them, Jim-Jim?"

The big Sandwich Islander caressed his knife point. "Z-z-z-t!" he answered, with a motion across his throat. Mike shuddered, feeling sick.

"Ha! Or . . . Wait." Bouchard's eyes swept them, tasting their fear and enjoying it. "Who will join me to serve the true and rightful cause of the Republic of Argentina and to kick the pig King of Spain in the eye?"

Mike expected all to refuse. He was wrong.

As he watched, three of the sailors stepped forward, repeating words of loyalty after Bouchard. It was too much. Mike groped for the rail and leaned over, his sick stomach cleaning itself. Men he'd suffered with—men who were supposed to help him warn Monterey—joining against all that was good! When he turned back, the three wretched deserters were being led away by a Malay and a Creole.

"Two traitors, a King-loving priest, and a baby!" Bouchard stared at the remaining four. He spat over the rail. "Jim-Jim! Over!"

The big savage moved like a panther, each hand darting out and catching the neck of one sailor. The splashes of the two bodies into the sea sent specks of water back over the rail.

Mike's nails were digging into his palms, and he could taste blood where his teeth were biting his lips. Sheer fury held him bound to the deck, unable to speak or move. Padre Serra backed a step and reached for his rosary as the Sandwich Islander turned toward the two.

"Wait." The voice was cool and amused, and Mike's eyes were pulled to a new figure that stepped out. His walk was easy, and his whole manner was casual. In the group, his relaxed quietness had made him seem neutral and unimportant; now he seemed almost the adventurer type Mike had heard his uncle describe in tales of his Irish ancestors. "Easy, Hypolite. The boy looks more Irish than Don, in spite of the Don clothes. And since my cabin boy died of scurvy . . . hm-m-m, perhaps I could use him. Boy, what's your name?"

Suddenly the fear and the futility disappeared. Mike felt his legs relax, until he seemed almost weak. Use him . . . take him along . . . to Monterey. They wouldn't know he could swim like a fish; most seamen couldn't. And in the night, if he could get to shore and find a horse . . . a little warning was better than none.

He cleared his throat. "Michael Obanion, sir," he answered. His voice shook a little, but it was sudden faint hope that caused the tremble now.

"See? A fine Irish name, that. Mike, me b'y, I'll make a very proper cabin boy of you, I will that—with a cat-o'-nine-tails, too, if needs be." The man laughed again, and it seemed more savage than the gesture of Jim-Jim.

Padre Serra was staring in horror at Mike. Mike held his face stiff until he could turn casually. He chanced a faint wink, and the priest frowned. Then Padre Serra smiled weakly.

Jim-Jim moved toward him, but the voice of the pirate stopped the advance. "Father, you're a priest. *Tú eres padre, verdad?* Good. And you're supposed to convert the heathen. Well, now, I have a fine lot of heathens, most of them half-converted, and they'd like a priest. I forgot to ship one on this trip!"

He translated it into halting Spanish, and Padre Serra nodded. "It is my duty to bring light to the savages—to convert them, yes. But I'll not lead them into pillaging against those who serve the gracious King."

"Fair enough, and amusing too, Padre. But suppose you convert them and *I* will do the leading. Jim-Jim, put them on the boat for the *Santa Rosa.*"

He swung to Bouchard. "About half my men fight better when they have a priest to absolve them before battle—and yours can use one too, Hypolite. I'll see that this shaven-pated priest does no harm."

Bouchard shrugged heavily. "Have it as you wish, Peter. But see your men do fight! We waste too much time on these. Now, we move against the King—for God and Country, eh?"

"For God and Country," Peter Corney, commander of the *Santa Rosa,* agreed with a grin. "Bring them along, Jim-Jim."

Mike felt himself being picked up and thrown over a bulging shoulder. Jim-Jim began lugging the two of them down the ladder, leaving them the choice of hanging on or falling into the sea. Mike felt an urge to bite the neck where the pulsing jugular vein showed.

But his eyes spotted a movement to the west, where the longboat from the *Boston Belle* was drifting. He was almost sure he saw part of a man's body inside the boat, lying at the bow and paddling with his hands, heading the boat toward the two unlucky sailors who had been tossed into the water and were attempting to swim away. It could only be Hawkins! It must mean that the mate had reached the abandoned longboat.

Then the motion ceased, just as Mike was dumped onto the bottom of a boat, and the big hand of Jim-Jim swung down, striking against the side of his head. Mike felt a moment of pain, and then he was unconscious. He hadn't seen enough to be sure.

They were under weigh when Mike came to in the filthy hold of the *Santa Rosa*. It was a rude awakening. The men around him had invented a new game—they were pricking him with a large pin, trying to see who could prick the deepest without bringing him back to consciousness!

It would have been bad enough without the petty torture. The hold was cramped and smelly, with filthy mats on the rough planking and hammocks crowded together above, strung from any support that would hold them. The cook had an improvised galley in one corner, and smoke from the fire on the stones only partly escaped through a porthole. Mike found that the food itself was unspeakable—bad meat, soggy biscuits, and a starchy paste from the Sandwich Islands called *poi* which had turned sour; there were other things which Mike could not even recognize.

The men were treated worse than pigs, and they responded by taking out all their hates on Mike, since he was forced to be with them.

Jim-Jim turned out to be the mate of the motley crew, and he was the worst.

There were about a hundred in the crew of the *Santa Rosa,* thirty from the Sandwich Isles and the rest a mixture of Americans, Spanish, Negroes, Portuguese, Manila men, Malays, and even a couple of English. The *Argentina* crew apparently were similar, though almost three times as numerous.

There was valuable information about the pirates here, and even though they tried their petty tortures on him, Mike was determined to learn all he could. When he escaped, his knowledge would be useful. He learned that the *Santa Rosa* had eighteen guns of twelve-pound and eighteen-pound sizes, and he filed that away with what he already knew of the strength of the crew.

Fortunately, Corney sent for him shortly after his return to consciousness. For a seaman, Bouchard's lieutenant was a fairly literate man. As soon as he found that Mike had been well educated, he loosened up and talked freely—so long as he was sure Mike was working himself half to death over the long-neglected cleaning, polishing and running errands.

He was particularly good at boasting.

"We're playing this the right way, me lad," he announced, the third day. "Yours wasn't the only ship to head for California before us. But we spread the word around that we'd be attacking Santa Barbara first. Here now—you call that polished!"

He reached out a lazy fist and caught Mike on the breastbone, sending him reeling. Mike bounced off the wall, shaking a head that was heavy with too little sleep in the stinking hold and too much work polishing Corney's navigating equipment. But he held his tongue. Corney pared his nails thoughtfully, grinning quietly.

"So the garrison down at Santa Barbara is shivering and waiting for us with all their guns ready. Let them shiver. We swoop down on Monterey, and before de la Guerra at Santa Barbara can think of moving his troops, we've sacked the capital of the King's precious Alta California, made off with the loot, and no harm done us. Clever, isn't it?"

It was. Mike knew that the soldiers at Monterey were too few and too careless. They'd had a quiet life and had been taking it easy. There was no chance for advancement for them, no salary after they'd spent their original grant of money, and no reason to think seriously of protecting the city.

It would be as easy as Corney thought—unless Monterey could be warned. Even with warning, it seemed almost hopeless.

"For God and Country," Corney said. "And don't you go thinking you can laugh at that, Master Obanion. It's God's service to be putting down oppression and helping a free nation get started against a bloodsucking King like Philip. The more damage we do him at Monterey, the better we serve a country that isn't too niggardly to accept citizens who can do it some good. Don't ever let me see you laugh at Argentina and freedom, me lad!"

Mike knew enough to be quiet. Corney nodded. "And the loot in Monterey—aha! None better since we sank the old *Royal Embrace* with the skipper's wife tied to the mast and screaming like twin banshees!"

Strangely, while he talked pure piracy, he really seemed to believe himself a loyal and worthy citizen of Argentina. Mike wondered— could that be the effects of this freedom they praised?

"And the burning—it will be something to see the Dons' city burning to the last stick and stave!" Corney interrupted his thoughts. "Now be a good boy and run down to the galley. I promised cookie you'd wash the slops when you were finished here!"

Mike went out, his head swimming. He tried to picture Monterey in flames, but it only made him sick deep inside. Looting had been bad enough, but sheer destruction was unheard of! He slowed, filled with horror. On deck he came face to face with Jim-Jim, who stared at him with a grin that showed the man's hope for an excuse to practice his little tortures. Mike straightened his weary back, pushed the fear and hatred from his face, and tried to move briskly.

He was surprised to see Padre Serra working over the stack of filthy dishes as he entered the galley. "For food," the priest explained. "This Peter Corney—the just God will see to him! He lets me bring the light of the true faith to the heathen for my life—and he then tells me I must work for the food to sustain that life!"

The priest stopped, staring with horror at the cuts and tiny scars on Mike's body. "They are veritable devils! Miguel, we shall yet bring them to justice. If your plan works, or if I can make even one savage see the error of his ways, and persuade him to escape to shore . . ."

Mike looked up in fresh surprise. He hadn't realized that the padre was trying to do that. If he were caught, it would surely mean the worst death Corney and Jim-Jim could devise.

But the priest only smiled at his protests. "No, don't worry, I'm being cautious. But I've learned that the ships are short of water and provisions. The crew will not fight on half rations. You see? Bouchard and Corney must stop somewhere first to take on supplies."

All the miseries of the past few days suddenly seemed worth-while. "Bless you, Padre!" Mike exclaimed. "And it will take at least a day to load those supplies. I'll have time enough, if I can find a way to sneak overboard . . ."

"Perhaps if I could find smallpox among the crew, or some other thing to hold their attention . . ." Padre Serra smiled bitterly as he scraped the dishes. "Now, go back to this Corney. Tell him I had finished here—surely God will forgive me the little lie, and your work is more important than this, while I can do very little else. Learn, Miguel—learn all you can. And pray!"

Mike was praying as he passed Jim-Jim, so hard that even the knife which whipped past his ear, barely nicking him, could not break his thoughts. For once, the Sandwich Islander got no satisfaction.

He was still praying as he carried Padre Serra's false message to Corney.

The man grinned. "Treacherous priest," he commented. "He thinks I don't know he's trying to spread treason. I've plans for him after the battle. . . . We'll see whether the boys fear his cross or my whip more. Mike!"

If Corney had discovered Padre Serra's plotting, might he not know everything? And if he did . . . Mike kept a straight face, though, hoping it was only a bluff. "Yes, sir?"

"Mike, what do you know of the Russians?"

"The Russians, sir?" Mike knew they had settled with their Aleut hunters at Fort Ross north of the Bay of San Francisco six years before. They had come to capture the Spanish trade in sea-otter skins with China and perhaps to establish a foothold for a claim of territory that should be Spanish. He knew little more, and could see no point to the question.

"Sure, lad, the Russians. They don't get along well with the Dons, do they?" Corney grinned again, propping his boots up on the table. "There's neat's-foot oil in the case there. And see that you do a good job, lad!"

Mike took as long as he could to find the oil, hoping Corney would go on talking. He stole a glance under his armpit, but the pirate was simply waiting, impatiently tapping his nails as Mike pretended to look for the oil. Mike knew he could hold off no longer. He made an exclamation at finding it and turned to the boots.

"Ah, that's a good lad. I'll make a seaman of you some day." The man smiled at the ceiling, and then glanced at Mike again. "So, if someone calls on the Russians, who among the Dons would know about it? No one, right?"

Mike nodded. "Right, sir!"

"Right!" Corney grinned. "So, when I told Bouchard we were short on supplies, where do you think I told him to get them? Right again. We're bound for Fort Ross, and the Russians. Hey, easy with that oil!"

Mike bent all his outward attention to the boots, but he kept his face hidden, afraid it might show some of his thoughts.

The Russian settlement, more than a hundred English miles north of Monterey, wasn't all he'd hoped for in a stopping point. It would be hard to find horses there, or get help, and it would be a long and difficult trip by land.

But among the Russians, the pirates might feel safer and relax their guard. Since it was all he could hope for, he had to make the best of it. Somehow, Monterey *must* be warned.

CHAPTER 4

On to Monterey

MIKE's only chance would be to get away
early, before much of the loading
could be finished; even that small
start would be too little, with every bit of
possible luck, unless the ships held over longer
than they expected. According to Corney,
they would anchor at Fort Ross in the early
morning, and Mike had told himself a thousand times that he must awaken before then;
in fact, he had kept himself awake for hours
convincing himself.

The sound of the anchor chain rattling down penetrated even the men's hold, and it was that which finally aroused him. He sat up, trying not to seem too eager. Through the tiny porthole, he could see some of the Russians already being rowed out in small-boats. Behind them, part of Fort Ross was visible.

It was a strange mixture of good and bad. The crude huts of the Aleut hunters with the drying poles for their fish and meat were in extreme contrast to the sturdy and business-like trading center. But after the long months at sea, the gardens caught most of Mike's interest. Being so far from the main Russian supply bases to the north, the traders were forced to grow most of their own food, and the whole settlement was adjusted to that necessity.

"Mike!" Corney's voice startled him, and he jumped to show himself. He had learned that Corney demanded promptness above everything else.

"Mike, you'll find a brown trunk in my cabin—under the bunk. Here, take this key. Polish up the cups inside—and I know how many there are, so don't think you can steal any. Put them out. These Russians like a big display. Make it look good. Then go down to the stores. . . . Well, what are you waiting for?"

Mike knew from that what would happen next, and it did. He was lucky to be allowed only half enough time to finish the job before he was sent off on another. They had dropped anchor at seven, and it was ten before Corney, Bouchard and the Russians finally ended discussions—but supplies were already coming on board from a number of boats; some of the trusted men of the crew had been sent to buy the most necessary things.

Then there was a further delay as the Russians came back to discuss some little trifle. Mike groaned with impatience. But for once, his luck seemed to have changed. Corney saw him, and swatted his hip. "Get out from underfoot, Mike. Can't I turn around without you gaping at me?"

Mike's feet developed a new burst of speed as he ran down the passage and up onto the deck. He almost tripped over Jim-Jim!

"You boy!" Jim-Jim was too busy to bother with any fancy touches. His finger indicated one of the holds, and his fist started to come around to back up the idea. Mike ducked. Jim-Jim pointed again. "Down. Stow."

Sick with disappointment, the boy dropped into the hold, where the cook was directing operations. He spotted Padre Serra working busily, and the priest seemed completely discouraged.

"All we can do now is pray, my son. And sometimes I feel that in this den of evil, even prayers are lost. We can only wait."

"We can't wait much longer," Mike said hotly. "Corney knows about your work on the crew. He'll kill you."

The priest sighed wearily. "Then he will kill me. Miguel, I would die gladly if I knew our missions were safe from this monster! Yet it is sad to think that the one man in the crew who seemed so sincere should go to Corney and tell my every word."

The pirates had done well. The supplies were of every kind. Eggs, oil, liquors and wines were among the stocks, in addition to staples. The cook had obviously been sampling too liberally, and Mike watched hopefully. Ordinarily, the man ate and drank like a pig and then hid somewhere to sleep it off. But this time, slow hours passed before he crawled behind some of the crates, still waving his gun and giving orders for Mike and Serra to carry out.

Then Mike had to wait until the crews bringing supplies aboard were gone. But the time did come, and he climbed up and onto the deck again. It was probably too late, but he still had to try the long trip to Monterey—if he could slip over the side.

His luck remained bad. Peter Corney was coming up over the side, obviously just returned from the village. The pirate yelled for Mike, and threw him another key. "Mike, you know the little cabin off mine? Fix it up, and step lively about it."

He was grinning in great good humor. As Mike started to leave, the pirate reached his hands down and brought up another person—a girl, and obviously Spanish by her clothes. She could hardly have been fifteen, but she was dressed like a woman, with her hair wound in a bun at the back and fastened with a high comb. The mantilla over her shoulders and the blue short-sleeved, loose gown were not too luxurious, but they were tastefully chosen,

even to the bottom fringe that touched her ankles. She carried a fan as if she had done so for years, and her bare shoulders showed a tan.

Then she was turning to face him, and Mike gasped. It was Maria Antonia Estrada, the niece of José Estrada, a mission soldier. She was the prettiest of all the young girls, though some claimed she was spoiled.

Mike ducked back, barely remembering in time that she must not recognize him—not when he was supposed to be all Irish.

Corney was laughing, and the girl was obviously scared. But she wasn't showing it much.

Mike ran ahead to the cabin. It was dusty with lack of use, but little else had to be done. He listened as he worked. From Corney's cabin he could hear the mutter of the man's voice, too jovial and too amused, but her words were so low that he couldn't hear them.

Mike had just finished when Corney came in. "Did you see the little beauty, Mike, me lad? Some of these Don girls now, they surprise you. Not fifteen, and something out of a fairy story. Well, she'll have all the comforts of home in this cabin, won't she? 'Miss Estrada,' I told her, 'nothing but the best for you!' How'd you think I found her, Mike?"

"I have no idea, sir," Mike answered, and for once it was the truth.

"You'd never believe it. She came prancing up and wanted to know if I was the captain of the ship. She wanted to be taken to Monterey, and had heard I was going there. Even offered to pay me for the voyage! Ah, Mike, life'll be the death of me yet. I haven't had such fun since we skinned that scared Maori and left

him out in the sun! I told her the ship was
hers, of course—but d'you know, I didn't have
time to stop for her mother. She came along
as meek as you please after we had a discussion
—about how I was stronger than she was."

He went off chuckling. Mike stood, torn
with indecision. He had his chance, but he
couldn't leave Maria alone in this company!
He was in no position to help her now, but an
opportunity might turn up in the future.

Then his doubts were settled by Corney's
voice. "Up anchor, you lummoxes! Lay into
that capstan! We'll be under weigh in ten minutes or I'll have exercise with the lot of you!"

The sound of men chanting as they walked
the capstan around mixed with the rattle of
the anchor chain. Mike was too late again!

Then Corney was back, heading for his
cabin. "Out of the way, Mike, me lad. I must
escort our little lady to her cabin. Be off with
you!"

Jim-Jim put him to work cleaning bits of
litter the men had dropped on the deck, occa-
sionally kicking him when he bent over. When
that work was done, they were well offshore,
much too far for even Mike to swim.

He slipped down to the cabins and hid in a corner. Corney came out of his cabin alone, leaving the door ajar, and went up on deck without looking back. Maria was not in the room.

Mike tapped softly on the other door. "Maria!"

There was a sniffle, but no answer. "Maria, this is Miguel—Miguel Boronda."

He heard her breath catch, and the door was suddenly opened. He slipped in and locked it behind him. "Sh-h-h. They don't know I'm Spanish. We were captured, Padre Serra and I." He gave her the story quickly, trying to skim over the loss of his uncle and Hawkins before the lump in his chest could catch in his throat and ruin his manhood by tears.

Her own story was simpler. She and her mother had secured passage on a small supply boat for San Francisco, and the storm had blown them too far north. The boat had been wrecked near Fort Ross, and the Russians had given them shelter, but refused to let them have horses or a boat to return. When she'd seen the ships, she'd slipped off against her mother's advice to plead with the captain to take them back to Monterey.

"And now this. Oh, Mike!" She gave his name the English version his mother used, as his few best friends in Monterey did. But there were no tears in her eyes. She was sick and scared, but her courage was holding up. "Help me, Mike! Help me!"

His voice caught as he promised all the help he could give. He knew he could do nothing for her, and suspected she knew it too. At least her mother was safe—if Monterey survived, a boat could be sent for her.

"And *my* mother?" he asked. He had been wanting to ask it long before, but had found no chance.

She shook her head. "She still has the fever, and she cries for you, Mike. But the doctors say she will live if you return. She . . . Mike, go quickly!"

Her ears had been better than his. Mike barely had time to close the door behind him before Corney was in front of him.

"So? A fine sneak you are, Mike. Can't turn my back on you." His hand came up, then paused. Mike prepared to dodge, but the pirate suddenly laughed. "Oho, so you took a good look at her, eh? Well, I don't blame you— but if I ever see you bothering her again, I'll drag you over the side a day and a night."

He dropped onto his bunk and stuck his feet out. "Off with my boots, Mike. It's been a hard day, but a pleasant one. Hypolite and I make a good pair, at that. Next anchorage, Monterey!"

Mike dropped the boot, but the man didn't notice it. "We anchor in the Bay, sir?"

"Right under the fort! No more nonsense."

This time Mike put the other shoe down quietly. There'd be no more stops, he repeated to himself. He had expected them to lay to outside the Bay for at least a night. It would have offered some chance. Now that was finished. He had failed, completely. Monterey would be looted without a word of warning. Padre Serra would probably be killed, and he and Maria . . .

"Go help Jim-Jim," Corney told him, rolling over on the bunk.

It should have sent shivers up Mike's back. The mate was always worse at night. But now he didn't care. He walked out automatically to face the petty torture of the huge Sandwich Islander.

Less than two weeks before, everything was so simple. He had had his worries, even then, over his mother and the pirates. But he had been heading homeward with the needed warning. Those troubles seemed small now, just as his present ones might seem very small shortly. But not now.

He choked, remembering his uncle calmly going back into the fire to do what could be done, while the others escaped. His uncle, who had been a second father to him, was almost certainly dead now. Even Hawkins, who had held his head up and kept him from drowning, must be dead. Mike's single glimpse was no proof that Hawkins had regained the long-boat; if he had, what could a man do against the sea in a boat that had no provisions?

After all that had happened and the worse things still to come, the cruelty of Jim-Jim seemed a very little thing.

Corney filled in the picture the next day, and Mike was present when Bouchard came over to the *Santa Rosa* in a boat for a final conference. He watched the two pirates muttering over plans and maps, and discovered sickeningly that Corney was only too familiar with the Bay. The *Santa Rosa* would anchor in a position to cover the landing, while the *Argentina* remained under weigh, to send in boats to assist in shelling the town and fort.

That night Mike joined Padre Serra in complete gloom. His uncle must be dead, his mother was dying, perhaps, and he was completely useless to everyone except Corney, the pirate. He was particularly useless to Maria.

In fact, he was unable to approach her cabin until the night when they sailed quietly into Monterey Bay, November 27, 1818, precisely at midnight. Corney was on deck, directing the anchoring and making sure everything was done quietly.

She opened her door at Mike's knock. "Maria, you all right?" he began.

"Yes, Mike," she answered, but her voice was frightened. "He treats me well enough; he pretends he's a gentleman and my host. But he's such a beast underneath! Mike, I heard the anchor. Where are we?"

"Monterey—below the fort!"

Her eyes widened, and she turned to him.

"Then, Mike, you can go. I know he won't attack until daylight. Even a few hours may help. Go—go at once!"

"I can't leave you here," he denied, though his own mind had been working on those few unexpected hours of grace. "If I can steal a boat from the deck, Maria, Padre Serra and I might manage it . . ."

"No!" She put her hand to his lips quickly. "No, don't think of it. You'd be caught. Only leave, try to escape. Don't mind me—all those others must be saved. And perhaps they can rescue me. Go, Mike. *¡Vaya con Dios!*"

He protested for a few moments longer, but he knew she was right. She blew out her candle to prevent any light from revealing the opening of her door, and her hand found and clutched his for a quick moment in the darkness. Then he was outside.

No one was about. He looked across the Bay. Over three thousand people, not counting the ranchers outside the city and the Indian servants, lay there unsuspecting of impending terrors. With the help of a moonless night, the enemy waited here unknown to them.

Mike slipped toward the rail, just as a figure moved in the darkness. It sounded like Corney's steps as the man moved aside.

Someone else joined him, and there was a muttered conversation. Mike looked at the other rail, but men were there too. He huddled behind a coil of rope, wishing that the

two would move on. He could slip over the side and they might not hear the splash of his dive—at least they couldn't follow him in the dark. But then they might simply speed up their plans and attack Monterey before morning.

Finally, one of the figures melted away in the blackness. The other stood there, smoking a pipe. A wisp of smoke reached Mike's nostrils, and he knew he had been right—it was Corney. The pirate was probably looking at the town and gloating over the easy victory he would have.

"Mike! Hey, me lad!" The words were low, but they caught the attention of the crew, and Mike heard his name passed on down the line. Corney stood a while longer. Then he swore briefly, and headed toward his cabin.

But now other troubles came up. Some of the crew seemed to be looking for Mike. They passed within feet of him, calling his name quietly. One fat little Malay almost stepped on him.

Mike drew himself closer to the rope, and he prayed. Either that helped, or he was just lucky. No one found him. Another half-hour passed, and the search was apparently abandoned—at least there were no further calls for him.

He slipped to his feet silently, and his hand found the railing. He'd have to undress in the water—there was no safety here. He drew himself up, measured the distance, and prepared to dive.

A hard hand suddenly gripped his shoulder, and he was swung around and up against an iron-muscled chest.

"Mike!" Jim-Jim's voice had a satisfied sound to it, as if nothing could have pleased him more. The pressure of the hand bit into his shoulder until he could barely keep from screaming.

Jim-Jim grunted again, and headed across the deck, half-carrying, half-dragging Mike with him.

Now he *was* in trouble! The big Sandwich Islander was heading for Corney's cabin. He'd tell about finding Mike in the act of jumping overboard, and Corney would need to know no more.

Mike tried to remember whether he had been in a diving position obvious enough for the man to notice. But it didn't matter. Jim-Jim could always lie about it, anyhow.

Jim-Jim knocked on the door, and threw it open at a barked word from Corney. The big mate muttered something in rapid Island speech, too fast for Mike to follow. The speech ended in a question, and Corney nodded.

Jim-Jim chuckled happily. His arms came up until Mike was suspended in mid-air, and his big foot moved sharply forward. The boy landed in the middle of the room, just as the mate's other foot caught him in the ribs.

CHAPTER 5

Battle in the Bay

WHEN the worst of Mike's agony had receded, Jim-Jim was gone. Corney sat waiting; his whole attention seemed to be focused on the light glinting on the blade of a large knife he held.

"It would seem that Jim-Jim doesn't like you much, Mike," he said in a calm, speculative voice. "I wonder if I do. Didn't you hear me call?"

Mike tried to evade the question. "I heard the men calling me, sir."

"I see." Corney thought it over and apparently accepted the answer. His voice took on the exaggerated patience of a man dealing with a stupid and misbehaving child. "But you gave no answer. You hid. You even tried to escape from Jim-Jim by going overboard. I suppose you have a good reason, lad? Or should I be opening your ears with this knife?"

Mike barely heard the threat. All he could think was that Corney hadn't guessed he was trying to carry a warning to the town.

"I thought you were asleep, sir," he answered, trying to keep his relief from showing in his voice. "I thought it was Jim-Jim who wanted me."

Corney frowned at the answer, started to speak, and changed his mind. He motioned with the knife. "Come here. Let's see that scrawny body of yours." He studied the marks on Mike's skin, and tossed the knife aside. "So. Jim-Jim is still playful, and you're afraid of him. Well, that's between you and him. But next time, when you wait for a second call, it will come as a knife between your ribs."

"Yes, sir."

"Yes, indeed, lad. Now then, can you handle a gun?"

There was no reason not to tell the truth that Mike could see. "I'm very good with one, sir."

"Good. Most of the crewmen are no good at all. In the morning, if needs be, you shall have a gun and we'll see what manner of man you are. Now be off with you."

On the deck, activity was going on under the direction of Jim-Jim. Mike took one look and knew that any further plans for escape would be useless. He might as well get used to being a future soldier for Peter Corney, expected to kill his best friends! He found his way to the straw pad where he slept, and was surprised to find Padre Serra waiting for him. The hold was asleep, and they talked in low voices, undisturbed. Serra had been working on the Catholic members of the crew; he had warned them that to fight meant to risk dying without proper final unction, at the risk of their souls. But they feared Corney more than God, it seemed.

It was not yet dawn when Mike was awakened to take Corney his breakfast of eggs and wine, but the man had obviously been up for hours. He ate on deck, watching the fixing of

the guns. "The Dons were warned," he told
Mike, pointing to the half-lit shore. "Santa
Barbara must have kept its troops at home, but
the local men have been doing little enough
sleeping, all the same."

Even in the dim light, it was easy to see that
El Castillo, the fort, was bustling with activity. The Bay of Monterey curved around
like a quarter-moon, and the fort lay about a
mile southwest of the city, located on a hill
where it could cover both town and Bay. A
battery of cannon was being manned now, and
other men were frantically at work all over the
hill. For a second, Mike's hopes rose. His
warning had not been needed.

Then he sobered, as he looked toward the
city itself. Everything was quiet, from the
Presidio where the Governor should be, to the
farthest fringes. Low adobe houses with empty
patios spread out in a half-circle from the
Presidio toward the hills behind the harbor.
Their red-tile roofs made a pretty picture
among the trees and shrubbery. It was a scene
of perfect peace—and desertion!

That left only forty underpaid and dis-
gusted men, half-loyal to the King and not at

all loyal to the local inhabitants, to defend Monterey—with a few volunteers, perhaps. Everyone had slipped off to the country, it seemed, to seek refuge among the outlying ranches, leaving only the militia behind, against over three hundred pirates!

Maybe Padre Serra was wrong, and the priests who felt the King was ruining them were right; maybe freedom was better. At least, from what he had heard in Boston, people had fought for it whole-heartedly during the American Revolution, instead of running away. Here, the King's policy of sending misfits and malcontents had been made worse by taxes and laws against trade that robbed the people of all incentive. What could a ruler six thousand miles away know of their needs—or care?

A shout from the shore cut through Mike's thoughts. He heard only enough to know they were hailing the *Santa Rosa,* and demanding a boat be sent ashore to discuss matters. Corney laughed, and yelled something back in insulting Spanish.

The *Santa Rosa* lay directly under the fort, with most of the American, Spanish and Portuguese members of the crew manning the guns. The *Argentina* lay farther out, with her boats already in the water. Now a strip of cloth went up her mainmast.

Corney nodded at the signal and turned to his men. "Fire!"

All eighteen guns thundered, rocking the ship hard over, and the fort shook under the rain of shot. But it was too high for much damage. Then puffs of smoke rose; an ugly whistle passed over Mike's head, and he ducked as a twelve-pound ball went through the rigging.

Mike suddenly realized he could be killed just as easily by his friends as by his enemies; shot didn't examine anyone's sympathies before killing him.

"Sensible," Corney conceded. "They have two batteries, and one is too high for us, I think. Elevate your guns! Fire at random when ready!"

The missiles were still too low to reach the second battery. And the guns up there were firing down again; the shooting was bad, since the King's soldiers had never had practice drills. But one shot hit the deck, opening a hole, and Mike's ankles suddenly felt as if a giant had struck his feet with a sledge hammer from below.

The *Argentina* was sending out more boats, all of them manned to the gunwales. Corney looked up at the fort and shrugged. "We'll have to land at Point Piños. We'll never reach the second battery with our shot. But we can take it from land. Mike, get a gun from supplies—then get the girl and bring her up."

"The girl, sir?"

"Step it up, me lad. I'm keeping my promise to set her down in Monterey. It'll do her good to see how Peter Corney handles her precious Dons. Lively now, Mike!"

Maria's white face showed her fright, but she walked with her head held high. The reports of the guns and the whistling shot were coming faster now, preventing any conversation. Mike led her up to Corney. The gun at his side seemed to give him new stature among the crew, who opened a way for him.

They had all been haggling with Corney, and Mike heard enough to know that they were demanding Padre Serra go along; they'd solved the problem of fighting without priestly comfort by deciding to make sure they had such comfort right at hand. Corney finally nodded.

"Bring your priest, then. Jim-Jim, you'll guard the King-lover. And you, Mike, see that the girl behaves. Into the boats, now."

A ball-shot came down near them as they climbed into the boats. If the fools on shore had used nails and metal shards, the shot would have caused trouble, but it only set up waves on the calm harbor.

Point Piños lay three miles to the west of the fort, forming one end of the horn-shaped Bay. Mike found his loyalty to the King falling rapidly as he saw how undefended it was. Year after year, the King's men had taken fortunes in hides, tallow, and sea-otter skins from Monterey; in return, there had been only a few old cannons, manned by unpaid soldiers. The men from the *Argentina* and *Santa Rosa* landed without trouble at the completely unguarded spot.

They began marching against the hill where the fort was located. Mike could see the men in the fort trying to move the guns to cover the landing, but there was no time. Only the light-

est artillery could be swung, and that meant
rusty old fieldpieces. Against the pirate forces,
the odds were all too uneven.

Bouchard ordered a halt at the foot of the
hill, and Corney assembled the nearly naked
Sandwich Islanders in front, armed with pikes
carrying wicked blades at the end of stout ash
poles. Mike and the better riflemen were to
stay behind. Padre Serra and Maria lay behind
stones, between Mike and Jim-Jim.

The mate grinned. "Mike kill lot men, Jim-
Jim like," he suggested. Having a gun had apparently made Mike a member of the crew,
instead of a mere cabin boy, and now he was
to prove his worth.

Maria and Padre Serra were praying for the unhappy people of Monterey, and Mike tried to follow it with his own prayers. But the ragged sound of a bugle cut in, and the pirates were away on a charge, yelling ferociously. Mike began firing with the others, seeming to aim at the fort, but placing his shots where he hoped no harm would be done. Luckily, most of the other firing went wild too.

The charge had barely started when the Spanish garrison left their guns and raced toward their horses. Mike watched with a sick feeling as they fled down the hill and away. A minute later, the pirates were hauling down the flag of Castile and running up that of Argentina.

One of the few lucky shots from the fort had drilled through the chest of one of Corney's Portuguese riflemen, but it seemed to be the only casualty to the pirates. Padre Serra started toward the dying man. Jim-Jim reached out to stop the priest, looked uncertain, and then let him go. After all, Serra was supposed to administer final rites. The big mate stood back, but kept a watchful eye on the priest, who now bent over the Portuguese.

The pirate died with a final convulsion of pain, and the padre rose slowly.

Suddenly a hoarse shout came from his throat. His arm lifted the crucifix and motioned it wildly toward the foot of the hill. "The tree—the big oak!" he cried.

Jim-Jim rushed toward him. Grabbing Maria's wrist, Mike charged after the mate. Before they could reach the priest, Padre Serra seemed to collapse over the dead pirate. His body shook, and he writhed, moaning and flailing at the ground with one fist. Jim-Jim hesitated.

"Loco," the mate muttered hoarsely, and there was a primitive fear of insanity on his ugly face.

Mike's heart tightened painfully in his chest. To see his one remaining friend . . .

A twist of the priest's body had brought his face toward Mike, and one of Serra's eyelids flickered in a quick wink. "The splendid horse, the glorious oak!" he cried, and began twitching violently.

Mike's eyes flashed down the hill. The oak stood where the crucifix had pointed before, and there was the half-hidden form of a horse beside it. Relief washed over him, along with doubts. The horse might be a means of escape, but only if they could reach it. And that would take more than a pretense of madness!

Men were gathering around the priest now, at a safe distance. The padre gave a final convulsive twist, and came to his feet—with a pistol in his hands! He must have spied it in the dead man's pocket and played the whole mad part to cover his getting possession of it.

Padre Serra suddenly charged forward, shouting again, heading toward the horse. The men scattered wildly, afraid that the mad

priest would kill them all. Mike let out a yell, still holding Maria's wrists. To the men, it must have looked as if he were charging after the priest to catch him, and even Jim-Jim moved aside a step.

Ahead of them, a small arroyo cut a shallow trench in the foot of the hill, and the padre dropped into it, with Mike and Maria hot on his heels. "Go, quickly!" Serra gasped. He turned north, firing the pistol in the direction of the pirates.

Mike dropped low, running south toward the big oak where the horse had been. In the confusion, there was a chance they might all escape by splitting up.

He saw the padre falter suddenly as a shot

rang out, and hesitated. But the arm of the priest waved him on, and Serra was running again.

Some of the pirates must have spotted Mike and the girl, and guns were coming up now. Mike fired, and saw one of the men fall. But most of them seemed not to realize that he and the priest had gone opposite ways.

The horse was still there when Mike and Maria reached the oak. It was a big dapple-gray gelding, one of the officers' mounts. It must have run off in the battle and gotten its reins tangled in the limbs of the tree that hung low over a pathway.

It shied as Mike caught the reins and began freeing them, but horsemanship was second nature to Mike, as it was to all in Monterey; the men spent most of their lives on horseback —even the poorest. Mike gentled the animal and swung Maria up in front of the saddle.

He was behind her in a second, kicking the horse into a gallop toward the town. The pirates were soon left far behind.

It was a splendid animal, with a deep chest, and a smooth motion that carried them on in its lengthened and extended stride. The trees seemed to rush past them, and Mike could hear the whistle of the wind in his ears.

Now they struck a pathway leading into the town, and the horse took his own head, leaving Mike's hands free to support Maria. He kicked the animal gently again, and it stretched out to its fullest speed.

He came to a bend in the trail, and almost charged into another mounted man. He was already overtaking the Spanish soldiers, fleeing from the pirates. A shout went up, and some in front wheeled back suddenly.

Mike suddenly realized that he was hardly recognizable now as the quiet, decently dressed boy they had known. He shouted back at the men hastily, calling the names of the ones he recognized, and they halted.

One of the soldiers rode toward him, hand on gun, but already beginning to smile. It was Feliciano Soberanes, with whose family Mike and his mother had lived. Soberanes was tall, thin-featured, and the best-looking man in the militia. His dark gray eyes warmed as he drew nearer.

"Miguel Boronda—we thought you dead! *¡Gracias al gran Señor!* And Maria Estrada!"

Soberanes turned his head and shouted up the trail. "Estrada! José Estrada!"

A moment later, Maria was crying softly in the arms of her uncle. Mike was surprised to find that he missed having her on the front of his saddle. But he was busy sketching his hasty story for them as they all swung down toward the town.

Feliciano Soberanes shook his head sadly when Mike asked about his mother. "Everything is so confused. She was gaining strength these last weeks—some new idea of Dr. Torres that she should eat green weeds! It was a miracle. Then word came from Comandante de la Guerra in Santa Barbara that Bouchard was coming and we should flee. Women, children—*and* Governor Pablo Vicente de Sola—fled back into the Salinas Valley. I do not know where your mother is now."

He hesitated. "She is safe, though," he added as he saw Mike's face pale. But Mike knew that it was only a lie to comfort him; Soberanes did not know whether she was safe or not.

He forced his worry down, and began telling the pirates' plans as best he knew them. They would use the fort to shell the city. After that, there would be riotous looting—and the city would be ruined and burned.

José Estrada dropped back to confer briefly with Soberanes. After a minute, he galloped off with Maria in front of him. There were some friends who had not yet moved from their home on a near-by ranch, and he intended to leave Maria with them. By traveling at a full gallop, he could rejoin the others.

They reached the town, a deserted and empty place. The Custom House seemed strange and dead without people in front of it. The outside stairways, open patios, and shaded streets seemed unreal, without the chatter of voices, and the town seemed to prove already that a way of life had ended.

Soberanes watched the soldiers trying to shape up, and his eyes were hopeless and weary. "What can we do?" he asked. "The men have no stomach for fighting—what has the King done for them that they should fight for his honor? Let the people flee and the place fall. Then we can all go back to Mexico, where Philip has a Governor with enough power to protect us."

"But this is the capital of all California!" Mike shook his head, unable to believe it was that bad. "If it falls, we can't hold the other cities. We'll lose California, and only the Russians will be here to claim it. We can't let them destroy the city completely."

"Who will fight for new taxes and new bans on trading with the world? Why should they? The people remember only that the King is destroying the missions which made California, and that nowhere can we save anything, while he gets richer by taxing and taking our trade. You have come home to evil days, Miguel!"

Mike stared about, trying to believe that this city which had been built in half a century from the wilderness could be destroyed at the whim of a few loot-hungry pirates. Only empty houses and silent streets met his eyes.

CHAPTER 6

The Capture of Monterey

THE guns from the fort began pounding at the town, which had never been built to withstand fire from her own guns. The first shots were close, and the following ones were coming closer. A shot from one of the cannon hit the wall above Mike. He ducked uselessly, and then had to jump madly to avoid the falling roof! A piece of tiling hit him in the back, just as another shot fell on the crumbling building. The whole wall seemed to fall on him, and he went down under a mass of rubble.

A hand found his and helped him crawl up. Soberanes stood over him. The air was filled with the dust of the dried-clay walls.

Soberanes was shouting orders to the soldiers and militia. It was already too hot for them here, now that the pirates had found the range. A soldier screamed as a shot took off his arm at the shoulder. Mike turned away, sick. When he looked back, two others were carrying the wounded man away.

They were still retreating, as they had been doing since Corney's first shot. One of the militia threw down his gun and ran off, crying that he had been shot, though no missile had been near him.

"Let him go," Soberanes ordered. "Maybe he's wiser than we are." He picked up the flintlock carbine. "Even the guns are so old they are useless. We need fieldpieces, and what do we have—carbines and pistols!"

José Estrada, who had just rejoined them, touched Soberanes' shoulder. "There are two field guns—behind the Custom House. Remember? From the big fiesta we held two years ago."

Mike recalled the celebration. The guns had

been brought down from the fort then, and nobody had bothered to wheel them back up.

"Get them," Soberanes ordered. "We can't stay in the town very long, but perhaps we can make things a little rougher for the pirates."

Mike joined Estrada and half a dozen others. They darted through the zigzag streets toward the center of Monterey, trying hard to keep under cover.

A twelve-pound ball burst through the rear of the house just ahead, gutting the whole building. It missed the little group, and they continued running. Another shot fell near by, and a woman's high-pitched scream came from

the building beside its target. A thin, hysterical figure ran out, hugging a bundle to her breast. She saw Estrada and the men, and rushed blindly off in the other direction.

Estrada started toward her and then stopped. "She's headed toward safety, at least, if there is any. Crazy fool! We tried to send them all off. Now she thinks we're the pirates!"

The center of the town nearest the Bay was in rubble already, but they found the two small six-pound fieldpieces, together with a few ball shots and some powder. The store-room had been broken open by a shot, but the ammunition was unharmed. The guns were rusty, but probably usable.

Estrada swore loudly when he realized they had forgotten to bring horses, but there was no time to wait. Four men to a gun, they began wheeling them back toward the big Presidio building. Twice they had to clear the streets of rubble, but they finally rejoined Soberanes, where he was desperately trying to make a stand.

They all rushed to the open court of the Presidio and began setting the guns up to fire on the fort.

"Duck!" Estrada's voice rang in Mike's ears, and he dropped to his face. Something moaned over him, and there was a dull, earth-shaking sound behind. He came to his feet with the others, shakily. But two soldiers remained lying where they were—the big ball shot had mashed their bodies together into one mass of horror.

The shot fell steadily, and the solid walls of the Presidio shook and threatened to crumble. But they were sturdier than the walls of the smaller homes, and were withstanding the fire. Soberanes got the guns in position, looking out through an arch. The pirates were still firing steadily toward the guns. Sooner or later, they'd score a hit.

Then one of the men yelled and pointed. Mike's eyes turned, and he saw two figures—probably Corney and Jim-Jim—heading a party of men out of the fort. The pirates were wheeling six fieldpieces!

Soberanes and the men began lining up their two guns again, while Mike joined the others who were firing rifles and carbines. His gun was a good one, of English make, though old. But he was used to loading powder, wad-

ding, and bullet into the muzzle, tamping the load down, and dropping to one knee into firing position quickly.

Beside him, the fieldpieces went into action. One scored a hit on the pirates, and Mike could see confusion. He reloaded and deliberately centered his sights on Corney. A man beside the leader fell—it was too far for accurate shooting at a moving target.

"Ammunition gone for the fieldpieces!" Estrada called suddenly.

Soberanes shook his head sadly. "All right, we might as well retreat."

Rifle fire was sniping at them as they crowded out of the Presidio. Mike reached for his powder bag and found it empty. He slung the gun over his shoulder and began creeping after the others. The hissing of rifle bullets near him was harder to bear than the sound of the shot from the cannon. He found himself waiting for the next whistle, with his hair prickling. When the sound came, it was worse.

Suddenly something bit at him, and his whole chest seemed to explode.

Shot!

Wild thoughts crowded his brain as he

dropped, tripping Estrada. Then he realized he wasn't dying. The pain was all in his side. He looked down and saw a hole in his shirt. The bullet had grazed along a rib, gouging out a short trough of flesh. It hurt terribly, but the rib wasn't cracked, and it seemed to be only a minor wound.

He got to his feet. One of the men with a small kit came back and fell into step beside him, trying to dress the wound as they walked. They managed to stop the bleeding.

Finally, they reached the horses. The animals were skittish from all the noise of the battle, but mercifully they had not been harmed. Mike mounted the gelding again, and fell into place.

They proceeded carefully as long as the buildings and trees hid them. Then Soberanes yelled, and they kicked their horses into a gallop. There was a distant yelling from the pirates, and more shots were fired, but they were almost out of range, and the mounted men made a harder target to hit.

José Estrada pulled up beside Mike, motioning to two of the other men. Mike reined in with him, turning to look back at the town.

Three of the pirates had apparently swung away from the others who were marching in. They crossed one of the little streets toward an imposing house. It wasn't hard to guess that they were planning to do a little private looting and drinking before the others broke ranks. Estrada lifted his gun to shoot, but he paused and then lowered it.

"Too far," he decided. "But we could use prisoners." The others nodded. He turned to Mike. "You can go on with Soberanes and tell him, or . . . perhaps you have a score to settle with your recent captors and would rather come with us?"

Mike didn't hesitate. He took half of Estrada's powder and began loading his gun as they rode. Some distance away from the house, Estrada stopped. They dismounted and went on foot the rest of the way. There was no sign of the pirates at first, but a moment later, loud laughter proved they were still there.

Estrada consulted briefly with the others. Their strategy would be simple—they'd go in quietly and surprise the pirates. Taking off their shoes, they crept in. The three Sandwich Islanders looked up from their drinking into four guns, and the capture was completed. It had been too easy to give much satisfaction to Mike, but he felt better. Even a tiny victory was a relief, after their bitter defeat.

The three older men threw the trussed pirates on the front of their saddles. Luck had been with them—no other pirates spotted them until they were again outside the town, and riding madly after Soberanes.

Soberanes told them they were fools to attempt it alone, but he looked pleased as he took over the prisoners. "You're a little young for a soldier," he told Mike a minute later, "but it's too late to change that. You've proved yourself, now, and we need every soldier we can get. The pirates have Monterey, but we can try to keep them from going farther. The least we can do is warn the ranches as soon as the filthy murderers move out of the town."

Their destination, which was to become their headquarters, was the ranch where Estrada had left Maria. It had been built on a low hill, unlike most ranch houses, and would give them a clear view of the town, three miles away. It was well stocked, and would provide shelter against the weather, since the fifty-odd remaining men could sleep in the sheds. More important, it lay between the city and the ranches along the Salinas River.

The rancher, Montiféo Robles, greeted them warmly, though his face was lined with worry. He had decided not to move his family, since he felt they would be safer near the soldiers, he told them. A moment later, he spotted Mike.

"The size of my son, exactly," he exclaimed. "Young man, go into the house and wash; my wife will have clothes for you that will be better than those rags."

Mike had forgotten that the ruin the storm had started had been finished by the work on the *Santa Rosa* and the battle. He blushed at his appearance, and then forgot it as he began scrubbing off the grime that covered him. The bullet sore stung as he washed gently around it, but it was smaller than he had thought. Most of the soreness came from the bruise on his rib.

His eyes were devouring the details of the little guest room. It had been too long since he had seen civilization. The bed with its springs of woven rawhide and its soft mattress was a dream come true. Maybe some day he would sleep on such comfort again. Then his eyes fell on a little pile of money, and he smiled. He was back in California, for certain; here hospitality was thorough, and no traveler was expected to leave without all comforts.

Boston, Mexico City, and the rest of the world he had seen had taught him that this had been a little paradise. The forty thousand Indians, who were legally minors under protection of the missions and actually servants, made gracious living possible for all. Nobody worked, other than the Indians, and everyone had servants. There had been courtly manners, dancing, the pleasure of the universal noon siestas, boating, fishing, hunting—all the trappings of Utopia.

Then he frowned. There had also been the matanzas, where the cattle were slaughtered and their carcasses left to rot, because only the hides and tallow could be smuggled out, since the King forbade outside trade. There had been the shipping of criminals up from Mexico City as colonists, and soldiers who had no pay beyond their food and a little *aguardiente* to drink. And there had been the growing war between the missions that had first opened up the country and the King who now considered them too powerful.

And finally, there were the pirates. Monterey could never be the same again.

Maria was waiting for him when he came out in his clean clothes. She was also clean and reclothed, and seemed shy and withdrawn. "I want to thank you, Don Miguel Boronda, for rescuing me," she began. Then she saw the hurt in his eyes, and some of her uncertainty vanished. She smiled. "Thank you, Mike."

He bent over her hand to kiss it. Usually, his experience with Boston and his uncle's ship had made him embarrassed about the older and warmer style of manners among the Spanish, but now it seemed right and natural. She tucked her hand under his arm and followed him, questioning him about the details of the battle, while her eyes envied his luck at being a boy who could do things, and not a mere girl.

Soberanes smiled at them, though the smile was bitter at the edges of his lips. "You make a much prettier couple than when I first saw you. Here, Mike, would you care to see what is happening?"

He handed a small telescope to Mike. The boy lifted it to his eyes, but he had to blink back the tears that came into them; it brought back memories of standing in the crow's nest of his uncle's ship. The hurt of his loss was still strong, when the rush of events left him time to think at all. He needed the gentle firmness of his uncle and the strong efficiency of Hawkins more than ever now.

When he looked through the glass, he saw only what he had expected. But seeing it and imagining it were two different things. The looting pirates were wandering about, using axes to break up furniture, and tearing up houses in search of treasure. Others were busy with the two-wheel oxcarts they had found, moving provisions and goods of every description to the shore, where they would go aboard the *Argentina*. It was a rich haul for the pirates—better than capturing some rich freighter—and safer.

Maria reached for the telescope, and he passed it to her after a questioning glance at Soberanes. She looked, her face growing sick. Then she gasped sharply.

Soberanes caught up the 'scope. His face

hardened, and he passed it to Mike after a single view of the scene.

In the glass, Mike saw that the pirates had found new fun. Three of the poor Indian servants had apparently hidden out in one of the houses, and the pirates had found them. Jim-Jim, or another man as heavy, was working on them with a whip.

"We can't do anything for the poor wretches," Soberanes said wearily. "Just as we can't do anything about anything. And down in Santa Barbara, Comandante de la Guerra is hanging onto every man he has. He's safe enough—your brave pirates won't attack an armed town. And we could have been safe enough, if some of the wealth taken from us to feed the court across the sea had been returned as a few more honest soldiers!"

"Couldn't de la Guerra send a few troops, at least?" Maria asked.

"Not enough; we're all too weak here in California. Yet, if he'd send word to us that some were coming, it would give heart to the men who are cowering with their wives, and it might even scare Bouchard away. If he even began to move his troops up, it might do the trick, without endangering him. But it's too late to think of that."

Maria got up, frowning—it was a pretty frown, Mike thought, but there was something strange on her face. She smiled at him briefly and headed toward the house. Mike got up to follow, but Soberanes held him back.

"You're a soldier now, Miguel Boronda," the man said. "I've got work for you. As soon as Estrada finishes organizing the watch schedule, all four of you who captured the pirates are to take them to the Rancho del Rey, where Governor de Sola is hiding—or carrying on the government, as he calls it. He's still the governor, and prisoners of war are his business."

"I was going to look for my mother . . ." Mike began. He cut it off, realizing how selfish the words sounded.

Soberanes smiled. "I'll get word out to search for her; the women are better at checking up on such things, anyhow. And you couldn't do much alone. I'd rather have you go along with Estrada—maybe seeing that a boy of your age is a good soldier will make some of the fools with de Sola realize their duty."

Mike had to agree that he could do little to trace his mother alone, and he smiled his thanks to Soberanes. Thinking of his mother, he picked up the telescope again. At least he could take one last look at the house where they had lived before he went on the trip with his uncle.

He was shocked. It wasn't a house any more. The walls had been broken by shot, and two pirates were finishing the ruin. As he watched, they came out with his mother's mirror, her most valued possession. One of them began cracking it up into small pieces to distribute among the Sandwich Islanders.

Mike dropped the telescope silently and went to find Estrada. He didn't want Soberanes to see the tears in his eyes.

Yet he knew it was only a small taste of what would come when the pirates decided to destroy Monterey completely. It began to look as if Corney's boast of burning the town to the ground would be easy to accomplish too.

CHAPTER 7

A Flag of Truce

At the Rancho del Rey, things were in worse confusion than they were at the improvised camp Mike had left behind. But it was a different kind of confusion. There it had been an attempt to stretch the facilities of Montiféo Robles to care for all the soldiers. Here it was a task of bringing order out of a group of confused men, who were all milling about the house hopelessly, not knowing where to start.

110

The man who finally listened to Mike and Estrada, after the first news had been devoured greedily, was more worried about where to hide the Governor's correspondence safely than about the prisoners. No, they could not see Governor de Sola—he was too busy trying to get couriers to demand help of Comandante de la Guerra in Santa Barbara.

Once the Governor stuck his head out of a hide-covered doorway and called somebody's name, but he was back inside before Estrada could reach him. His assistant stopped only long enough to tell Estrada that he'd have to wait—and why didn't he watch the matanza meanwhile?

"Now?" Mike asked, incredulously.

"Why not?" Estrada answered, since they were alone again. "It's crazy enough here for anything to happen. Probably half of the ranchers think they're too far for any danger."

They heard the sound of guitars then, and moved around the buildings. The great slaughtering of cattle known as a matanza was definitely going on, just as if Bouchard were still in Honolulu. They passed a group of men and women dancing the fandango, while others were standing around a great barbecue pit, stuffing themselves and gossiping pleasantly about the success of the party. A lassoing contest had just finished, and the serious work behind the celebration was beginning again, as the *nuqueadores* each began slaughtering the cattle being herded in with expert knife blows in the necks of the unhappy beasts.

Estrada shook his head. "The Governor's party expect to be killed tomorrow, and these people pretend there is no trouble. Let's try again, Mike. Someone may be a little less insane."

They finally found one man who agreed to take the prisoners off their hands. He had the pirates placed together in a room, still bound, and promised to bring the matter to the Governor's attention.

"The men," he asked, "what are they saying of the Governor?"

"They say he ran away," Estrada told him flatly.

The other nodded sadly, and his eyes grew even sadder as he glanced back toward the group watching the matanza. "I guessed as much. But what would you have him do? If he had stayed, would it have helped? You have been near the battle, in it, that is. Unlike these fools who dance and laugh, you have seen the danger. You know that this monstrous Bouchard would like nothing so much as to capture the Governor. The traitors in Argentina would reward him handsomely for that."

They agreed with him that the Governor had done the right thing. Mike suspected that it was probably true, though it would be hard to explain it to men who had fought hard, but now saw their homes being destroyed.

"Tell me," he asked the man, when business was finished, "have you heard of the Señora Boronda? She was sick, and no one knows where she is. She's my mother."

The other shook his heard sympathetically. "I know nothing of her. But if we hear, I'll try to get word to you."

Mike thanked him, and they left for the long ride back to the ranch of Montiféo Robles. The boy was beginning to feel saddle-weary; it had been too long since he had ridden. Also, the day had been one of constant strain, danger, and disappointment, and it was beginning to tell on him.

Soberanes was asleep when they reached the ranch, but one of the soldiers coming back from guard duty nearer the town directed them to a shed where they could sleep.

Mike dropped onto a pile of straw and began to remove his shoes. But it was too much effort. He fell back onto the straw and was asleep at once.

Soberanes was having breakfast when Mike awoke, and the man invited the boy to join him. It wasn't fancy—thick slices of fresh beef, plain bread, and a little fruit. After the filthy food on board the *Santa Rosa,* though, it tasted superb to Mike. He realized that he had forgotten to eat during the whole of the day before—few people had thought of food then.

"No news of your mother, yet," Soberanes told him gently. "We found one of her servants, but the Indian woman only knows that your mother was taken from the town in an ox-cart. I've also spread word that you're safe, which should cheer her, if she hears it."

Mike thanked him. Then another thought crossed his mind. "The padre—Padre Serra? Where is he?"

Soberanes looked surprised, and Mike recalled that he had forgotten to tell how they escaped, or that the padre had escaped at the same time. He recounted the events quickly.

"No one has heard of him," Soberanes said. "I'd have known of it, if they had. Either he is still hiding or the pirates recaptured him. But I think not—we saw them burying two of their men yesterday, and there was no priest with them. Wouldn't they have forced him to hold services?"

Mike tried to think so, but he couldn't be sure. They might have killed the padre, instead. He added Serra to the others he had lost in such a short time—his uncle, Hawkins, Padre Serra. It was almost better not to have friends and loved ones; then they wouldn't bring so much heartache when they were taken away.

One of the soldiers on guard duty came riding in at full speed and yanked his horse to a stop before Soberanes. "Pirates coming from the city, heading this way," he reported. "Only a few, but more may be coming."

Soberanes reached for the telescope and put it to his eye. "Four, six, eight, ten—eleven of them. Maybe it's a trick. But we can handle eleven easily enough, without waking the men who are asleep. Spread word, and bring horses."

About fifteen of the men joined Soberanes as he mounted. Mike swung up on the gelding, and groaned. The long ride the day before had left him one solid ache. He tried to rest his weight on the stirrups, but that didn't help much. He hoped it would be easier after a few minutes of riding.

They walked their horses down the trail to Monterey, stopping now and then while Soberanes searched with the telescope for a sign of ambush, or a general charge from the town.

Finally, when the pirates were half a mile away, the eleven stopped, facing Soberanes. The man in the lead lifted a scrap of cloth on a pole and waved it.

"White flag—must want to talk," Soberanes guessed. "At least, we know they don't want to surrender. Here, give me your knife."

He took it from one of the men. At the side of the road stood a small sapling, and he cut it off. His own handkerchief at the end served as a fair flag, and he waved it in the air.

The pirates seemed satisfied. They began

marching forward again. Soberanes proceeded more cautiously than ever now.

Mike had been staring at the leader of the pirates, and now he recognized him. "Jim-Jim!" Without thinking, he began to raise his gun.

"We accepted truce," Soberanes told him severely.

Mike lowered the gun, feeling his face flush. Soberanes had a right to reprimand him. It would do no good to start breaking his word, just because the pirates might break theirs. It would make him no better than they were.

Jim-Jim halted when they were fifty feet apart, and Soberanes motioned his men to dismount. "Say your piece," he ordered the pirate.

Mike shook his head. "He only speaks his own language—he can't speak English well, even."

"I speak Spanish, you little goat of a bad odor. May your ancestors . . ." Jim-Jim snapped.

"Enough," Soberanes cut in. "You speak Spanish. Speak it about your business."

Hate filled the eyes of the pirate mate, but

his teeth flashed in one of his twisted smiles. With his eyes on Mike, he brought his hand up across his throat. "Z-z-z-zt!" he said, exactly as he had done when Mike first met him. Then he turned to Soberanes.

"Hypolite Bouchard and his lieutenant, Peter Corney, officers in the free navy of the Republic of Argentina, have sent me under flag of true to deal with you in the name of God and Country. You have killed three of our men. They are dead, and we will forget them. You have taken three of our men as prisoners. We want them back."

"In the name of God and the King, you have my permission to want them," Soberanes answered him. "But to get them is another matter."

Jim-Jim scowled. "Then I am to tell you that you have three days to consider it. At the end of the third day, if they are given to us, we shall depart without further damage; if the men are not returned, we shall burn Monterey to ashes and begin moving into your country, burning all we find."

"And if we were to return them, and you decided to break your word to us . . .?"

"At least there is a chance," the pirate pointed out. "Return the men, and we leave. We of the free navy of the Republic of Argentina have more important work than killing men who fight like women!"

Soberanes shook his head slowly. "It's no use," he told the pirate. "We don't have the men. They're the property of the Crown, and of the King's representative. I can send word of your demand to him. Beyond that, I can make no bargains with you."

"Then send it. And when you return the men to us, send this skinny traitor with them, or it will go badly with you. I have use for him." He was pointing at Mike.

"The boy stays with us," Soberanes told him firmly. "Was that part of your message—or your own idea?"

Jim-Jim fingered his scar and again made the gesture across his throat. "It will be the wish of Bouchard and Corney when I tell them the young pig is still alive! We thought the mad priest killed him and the girl when he escaped."

He swung on his heels with a threatening look at Mike. The boy hardly saw it. He was too busy thanking God that Padre Serra was still free. Jim-Jim wouldn't have spoken as he did if they had recaptured the priest. He felt slightly better as he swung back onto the gelding.

Then Jim-Jim wheeled, with a wicked pistol in his hand. It was pointing straight at Mike. The grin tightened on the ugly face, and the gun spoke sharply.

Mike jerked back. He felt the wind from the bullet across his arm, but it missed. Something broke behind him. It was the telescope that had stopped the bullet, and now it lay broken in bits.

Soberanes' horse lunged forward, striking

the pirate's arm with its hoofs, and Soberanes brought his gunstock down on Jim-Jim's wrist. The pistol hit the ground. It had happened too quickly for the others to lift their guns, and now their leader was at the Spaniard's mercy.

Jim-Jim squeaked in fear and agony. "Guns on you. Corney is covering us from the city. You can't kill us!"

"I wouldn't try to," Soberanes told him. "You're still under your truce—but another false move, and you'll be dead under it. March!"

He prodded the pirate mate with his toe, and Jim-Jim almost fell on his face in his haste to escape. The others went with him, staring back sullenly. Soberanes watched them out of gun range before turning back. It was safer to risk the guns from the town than to trust the half-savages under Jim-Jim.

"It might be better to give up the prisoners," one of the men suggested, as they started back.

"They'd still burn the town," Mike stated, remembering the plans he had heard.

"It doesn't matter," Soberanes said, and disgust was thick in his voice. "They're in the hands of Governor de Sola now, and he'd be afraid the King wouldn't like losing prisoners. We can't hand them back, even if we want to. We'll have to wait, I suppose, and watch them burn our homes to the ground—and without even a telescope to see it better!"

The loss of the telescope had been important, Mike knew. With it, the sentries had been mere added precautions. Without it, they would have to station men near the town to watch, and even that wouldn't be as good.

It seemed hopeless. The pirates could slip out in small parties to raid and burn the whole valley of the Salinas, and they would go almost unchecked in the city. Sooner or later, of course, something would have to be done against them; Bouchard couldn't simply take over without opposition, even though resistance was sure suicide. Something would break, with all the pressures, and Mike shivered when he tried to imagine which of the possibilities it would be; none seemed at all good.

He prayed softly that Padre Serra was safe, at least. Perhaps the priest had decided to go to the mission at San Miguel. At least Mike could hope so.

They returned at a steady canter to the camp at the Robles ranch. Most of the soreness had left Mike, and he had time to wonder what Corney would think when he found he'd trusted an enemy and been fooled enough to give him a gun—a gun that Mike still had.

Shouts went up as they neared the buildings of the ranch. Men were milling about, with the center of confusion a crying Indian girl. Soberanes spurred forward, just as José Estrada started running toward him.

The woman was wailing so loudly that Mike could hardly hear the words Estrada was calling.

Soberanes shouted for attention, and someone put a hand over the girl's mouth and led her away.

"Now what is it?" Soberanes asked.

"Maria," Estrada answered. "She's run off to the town!"

Mike's heart dropped, and he stumbled as he was dismounting. "She couldn't!"

Estrada nodded. "She did—we just learned of it—the Indian girl was just telling us."

Soberanes sent for the girl. She was brought back, but it was hard to follow her words, because of the sobs that shook her. Gradually the story came out.

The night before, Maria had ordered the girl to pack a lunch for her in the morning, and to wake her before dawn. The servant had done so. Señorita Maria had dressed quickly, and started off with the lunch. When the servant started to follow, Maria had ordered her back. She had said she was going back to the Estrada house to get her dresses and her jewelry, and that she would return as soon as she could.

"That was this morning, before sunrise," Soberanes said. He put his hand on Estrada's shoulder, restraining the man's impatience. "Why didn't you tell us at once?"

"She told me not to tell," the girl answered, crying even harder.

She'd gone back to the house, and finally begun worrying. Then, instead of consulting someone else, she'd hidden in the girls' quarters. It was only after Estrada started looking for Maria that Montiféo Robles had hunted her up and pried the story out of her.

"The little fool!" Soberanes shook his head, frowning.

Mike tried to tell him that Maria was no fool, but his throat was glued shut, and the words wouldn't come. Maria must have had some reason. He was remembering the look on her face the day before. Something had been on her mind, and it hadn't been clothes. She had too much sense for that, and she had certainly seen what the pirates were like.

Estrada tugged impatiently at Soberanes' arm. "I ask permission to look for her."

"I'll go with you," Mike told him hoarsely. He lifted his foot to the stirrup. Estrada was already running toward his own horse.

Feliciano Soberanes stopped them with a sharp cry. "No! You do not have permission to go. You're soldiers, and you'll stay where you're needed."

He shook his head sternly. "Both of you. And that applies to anyone else who wants to rescue her." His voice softened. "You couldn't help her. The girl is gone. I'm sorry for that, too, José—I know she was almost a daughter to you, and I know you loved her. But I can't let two men face certain death to save a girl who is either captured or killed by now."

Estrada dropped his head, and stepped back

from the horse. He nodded reluctantly. "You are right, of course, Feliciano. God have mercy on Maria Antonia Estrada!"

Mike looked at Soberanes again, and knew it would be useless to protest. Probably the officer was right, and perhaps Maria was dead. He could never convince Soberanes to let him go after her.

Why had she gone? The question pounded through his head, but he could find no answer. It was like asking why the wind blew. There was a reason, but he couldn't know it—unless he could find her to ask!

CHAPTER 8

"Burn the Town!"

NOON came and went. Mike had hidden his determination, and had gone on as if he had never heard that Maria had left. But his decision was set. Even if Soberanes was his leader now, his first duty was to the promise he had made Maria; he had agreed to help save her from the pirates before he had joined the militia, and as long as she was in danger, he had to go after her.

Mike had tried to lay plans, but they were still vague. He knew that it would be impossible to sneak up on the town during the hours of daylight. The pirates would see him long before he reached the outskirts, and they would be waiting for him. He could give Maria no help that way.

By now, she must either have found some place to hide or have been captured. If she were hiding, then she might be able to steal back during the night. A party of men would be seen, but a single figure might slip past their guards.

Mike knew that he had to wait. It would be doubly foolish to go into Monterey just as she returned to the camp. He had to wait until it was dark, and then wait still longer until he could be sure she was not coming back.

He prowled about, trying to fill the long day with something that would be useful. The hours dragged, and he could feel the suspicious eyes of Soberanes on him; the leader wasn't entirely fooled by his apparent acceptance of orders.

Mike was grateful when his turn came to act as observer on the town. Soberanes teamed him with Estrada and two others to replace a group that had been out since morning.

They halted, half a mile from the pirate-held city, and took shelter behind rocks, where they could see without being fired on. The looting was still going on, but it was without system now. Pirates wandered into houses in groups and came out bearing loot. What they couldn't take, they smashed. And most of them were busy with sharp instruments, tearing apart the walls and floors in search of the jewels they thought the Spanish might have hidden there.

It would have been impossible to pass through the pirates, and Mike was glad now that he had been stopped by Soberanes. He thought of letting Estrada in on his plans. Two men, however, would have less chance of getting through than one. Estrada might even want to tell Soberanes. Finally, he decided against it, and tried to concentrate on simply watching the town. He tried to map a route toward it and through it that would be safest, though he knew luck was more important than planning.

He noticed that most of the pirates were growing bored with their looting by now, and that was a good sign. They might be more savage if they caught him, but they would pay less attention to what went on near them. It would have made it easier for Maria to slip through and hide from them too.

It was almost night when their relief came and Mike and the other three went back to the camp.

Soberanes sent for Mike at once. There was still suspicion on the officer's face, but there was pleasure too.

"Your mother has been found," he announced at once, and his smile flashed out at Mike. "She's doing very well, though of course she was worried about you. Now she knows you're safe, and feels better."

Mike dropped to a seat, trying to thank Soberanes. But the man waved it aside. "There's still more news. Your uncle isn't dead; in fact, he's with your mother. The same ship that brought the news of Bouchard to Santa Barbara found his boat—he got away before the ship sank—and took him along. He came up with de la Guerra's courier, when we first got the news, but nobody noticed him. The news of the pirates took all our attention right then, I guess."

Mike shook the first amazement out of his head.

"You must be lying to make me feel better," he said faintly. "Uncle Roger would be here fighting."

Soberanes took no offense. He smiled more deeply. "He would be, except that the long ride from Santa Barbara opened a wound in his leg which he got during the storm at sea. But that's healing again. You'll have a letter from him tomorrow. And he and your mother are coming to see you in another day or two. Pirates won't keep them away since they know you're here. Now do you see how silly it would have been for you to get yourself killed chasing after a girl, just when your family is found?"

He listened to Mike's thanks this time, but denied he deserved them. It had been the womenfolk who had discovered where Mike's mother was staying and had brought the story to the camp.

Mike ate a full dinner, alternately happy over his mother and uncle and miserable because Maria was probably in danger. Padre Serra was still unaccounted for, and Hawkins remained on the list of those lost; but he was learning to be grateful for what good there was, without bemoaning the fact that everything wasn't perfect. After dinner he found an excuse to work on his saddle near the trail from Monterey. Darkness had fallen an hour ago, and Maria might be coming back at any minute.

His eyes ached from staring at the trail, but there was no sign of her. At nine, Soberanes ordered him to bed, but he had managed to rip a seam in the saddle deliberately, and used that as an excuse to stay up.

He worked as slowly as he could, but nevertheless, it was finished by eleven. This time, Soberanes refused to be put off. He made it a formal order, and went in personally to see that Mike followed the command. "Can't have you looking exhausted when your mother and uncle come," he explained good-naturedly. "Now you get your sleep, young man."

He started to leave, then stopped. "I thought we'd found Padre Serra, boy, but it turned out to be false. There's some man hiding in the town—our scouts have seen him twice, sneaking about. But they say it's too big a man for Serra. Probably some deserter from the pi-

rates. Don't give up, though; a lot of lost
people turn up well enough, you know."

Mike knew he meant Maria as well as the
priest, and tried to smile. Then he rolled over
and peeked through almost-closed eyelids. Soberanes was still standing there, but at last the
man seemed satisfied, and Mike heard his foot-
steps leaving. It was almost a quarter after
eleven. Maria certainly wasn't coming back.

He rolled over again, peering about cautiously. Soberanes was gone, but some of the
other men were sitting up, attending to their
guns or talking softly. The candles burned out,
but the talk continued for some time longer.

It was worried talk. The men were gradually
realizing that their position was hopeless, and
that no help would come from Santa Barbara.
They were cautiously debating desertion before the pirates swept out from the city and began ruining the whole country. A few believed
in fighting, but to most of them such sure
death was not welcome. California was surely
doomed—there was no sense in fighting for a
lost cause.

Mike groaned softly to himself, realizing
again that the breaking point was near and that

something must happen soon—but that it almost surely would be utter disaster, whatever form it took!

At last there was only the sound of snoring. Mike slid off the straw softly and dressed in the darkness. He had spotted where one of the men had dropped his pistol and ammunition. With groping fingers, he finally located them and stuck them in his belt. One of the men rolled over, and Mike's heart seemed to stop. But the snoring continued again.

He reached the doorway and shoved back a corner of the hide that covered it.

There was no sign of Soberanes. The men were either asleep or out of sight. Mike studied the trees, mapping out a course that would keep him under their shade in the deepest darkness. He had considered taking a horse, but rejected the idea. With a prayer on his lips, he began the journey.

He was half a mile along the trail before he could breathe easily. He was away from the camp. Now he could see any of the soldiers who might be returning from guard duty; all he had to worry about was passing the pirate sentries.

Once he almost ran into a guard group of the Spanish soldiers. They were near the trail, where he had not expected to find sentry stations. But he heard their voices in time, and went around them.

Finally he was on the outskirts of Monterey. Most of the pirates were asleep or drunk, but a few were moving around, carrying burning pine knots for torches. He felt safe as long as he made no noise and clung to the darkness.

He tried to plan the best course toward the Estrada home, and began to feel almost sure he would make it safely.

A stone ruined his hopes. It rolled under his foot and fell against a board, making a sound that seemed thunderous in the silent city. Mike ducked back into the doorway of a ruined house, hoping no one had been near.

His luck was bad. A thick voice muttered, and another joined it. Torchlight appeared around the corner of the building, and Mike moved back into the second room of the little house.

"Heard a sound, I tell you," the first voice was saying. "Maybe that fellow who's been hiding from us—or somebody's found treasure, getting it out when we can't see."

"Just a rat . . . see, just a rat." The other voice was even more fuzzy than the first. Mike recognized it as belonging to an English ruffian under Corney. "Wanna sleep. Come on in here, get some sleep."

Mike darted farther back in the room as they stumbled into the house where he was hidden. A weak light came through from their torches, and he saw a chest lying on its side. It was barely big enough, but he squeezed into it, just as the two men entered the room.

"What's in the chest?" the first man asked, a touch of greed in his voice. "Let's see."

"Nothing. Nothing. I was here before, looked in it then. See, thought I remembered we'd left a bed here. Good place to sleep."

"Too near the wall. Walls have rats."

The Englishman considered it. "We'll move the bed, then," he decided.

Mike heard it scraping over the floor. Finally, the men were satisfied, and the bed creaked as they climbed onto it. In five minutes, they were both snoring loudly—one falsetto, the other like a blown conch shell. Mike shoved at the lid of the chest, and found his fears were justified. It moved a bare inch before striking against the legs of the bed. The men were too heavy to move, and the back of the chest was against the wall, neatly trapping him.

He lay there cursing his luck and worrying about Maria for at least an hour, but his body was growing philosophical. No matter how much his mind worried, it demanded and got its sleep.

Daylight was peeping through a crack in the chest when the awakening grunts of the two men broke Mike's sleep. He waited for them to leave. They seemed to take forever, until one remembered something about Corney having a meeting. They tottered out then.

Mike's body was stiff and sore from the cramped position, and the bed was hard to move. But finally the lid came out far enough for him to crawl out. He stretched himself, working off the cramps in his muscles. At last, he moved stealthily to the doorway and pulled the tanned leather hide aside a bit.

But he was still trapped. Outside, the pirates had apparently established a loading station for their loot, as well as a place to cook their lunch. There were at least a dozen of them there.

It was the longest day of his life. Twice men started toward the house, but both times they changed their minds. It must have been one of the first places to be looted. His stomach reminded him that he hadn't eaten, but there was nothing he could do about that. The long morning crawled around to noon, and thirst began to choke him. The longer afternoon crept on second by second. When night finally came, the cook fire was too bright, and he had to wait for that to die down.

This time he was more careful as he came out and moved stealthily along the streets. He put his feet down gently and listened for a sound from the men.

Mike found the Estrada house at last, looking as if it had been untouched. It had been small, and the soldier had been too poor to make it worth looting. Mike listened for sounds from within before entering. He debated calling Maria's name.

Steps sounded from down the street. He flattened himself behind a tree.

"All the gold's with the Governor," were the first distinguishable words as three men came nearer. "We'll strike it rich there. Bouchard has given orders to burn the town before morning..."

Another voice cut in. "Before morning! What do you think we're being called back for now?" In the light of the torch, Mike saw him raise a bo'sun's whistle to his lips and blow an assembly signal. He dropped it and went on. "Soon as we get the men together, we fire the whole place."

"Anyhow, we get good looting when we go down the valley. The ranchers must have plenty—look at all the cattle they keep. And when we get to this ranch where de Sola is— um-um! That's for me!"

The other laughed, after blowing his whistle again. "I hear Bouchard's going to make the Governor dance this here fancy-dangle all the way back to the ships."

They moved out of sight. Mike slipped from behind the tree and started to enter the Estrada house again. Maria had to be there now. She hadn't been captured yet; he kept telling himself that, over and over. Mike could no longer spare much time to look for her, though. The news was too important, and he had to get back to Soberanes with it.

The blow-up he'd expected was about to begin—and it was the worst of all his ideas. He shuddered at the thought of the pirates looting up and down the valley, even where his mother might be. They had to be stopped, but there was no way to stop them.

Mike slipped into the house. There were three small rooms, and he hurried through them, calling Maria softly. A faint light came in through the small open slits that served as windows. He moved along the walls, trying to use the windows as a point against which her outline might fall. But he already knew it was useless. She would have recognized his voice.

Shouts went up from outside. "Burn the town! Burn—burn—" The pirates were using it as a rallying cry. They sounded happy about it, as children were about a bonfire. Mike went to the door again.

The pirates were apparently converging on this section for a final look for treasure. They entered each house as they passed, yelling back and forth. Then he realized they were being systematic, as if they were looking for something definite. Had they seen him?

It was already too light to escape by the front entrance. He dashed to the back and saw it would be no better. Pirates were running down the street, and this whole section seemed to be a focus point for them. Some light from outside came through the slits in the walls, and he looked for a place to hide, but the rooms offered little hope.

He wondered which room would be safest. None, probably. The pirates would go through them all. The only chance seemed to be under one of the beds—they might forget to try the obvious. But it wasn't much to hope on.

Then memories came to him. He'd played with Maria when they were younger, and she had used one nasty trick on him in a game of hide-and-seek. There was a cistern that opened inside the cooking room, with a big wooden cover over it. It had been all Maria could lift when she was eleven, but it could be swung aside. Beneath it there were wooden timbers that braced the top of the cistern. It would be an awkward and unpleasant place to be trapped, but there was no other.

Steps were already coming near the house, and the pirate yells were louder. Mike heard a crunching of dry dirt outside. He wasted no more time. He ran for the cistern. The top was still heavy, but he was stronger than he had been as a boy, and it came up quickly in his arms.

Holding it above him, he lifted his legs over the side of the cistern and felt for one of the timbers. He shifted his weight and brought his whole body inside.

He was just lowering the lid when the steps

began to move through the front room, toward his hiding place. But the lid was down and he was safe before he could have been seen. The lid cut off the sounds from above. He could not tell what the searcher was doing. But for the moment he was safe.

CHAPTER 9

Trapped in the Flames!

THE sound of his breath was sharp in his ears in the hollow chamber around him, but he wasn't worried; the cover would keep that from being heard outside. He relaxed and sighed—to realize suddenly that it wasn't his breathing he had heard!

His hand darted out, to meet soft cloth and the small rounded arm beneath it. "Maria!" It could only be the girl—no one else would have known of the hiding place, or had any need to use it.

144

Hands grabbed for him in the absolute darkness, and her breath rushed out suddenly in a whisper. "Mike! Oh, Mike!"

She was trembling as he drew her closer to him along the slippery timbers. But there were still no tears as he touched her cheeks. Maria Estrada had courage. She wasn't like so many girls he had seen, crying over everything.

"Why'd you come back?" he asked softly. He should say something to comfort her, he knew, but he could think of nothing else, except the thirst that was growing worse with the smell of water below.

She stumbled over her whispered account, her breathing growing quieter as she went along. "I had to get a piece of paper—a very important piece of paper! It was dark, and I knew the pirates couldn't see me if I went carefully. My aunt had put the paper away, and nobody else knew where it was, so I had to come. And I found it too! But it grew light too fast, and I had to stay here. Then the pirates started going up and down, hauling things away. Last night I tried to leave three times, but they were all around here, singing and celebrating. I had to stay hidden."

She caught her breath again. "I was trying to go a little while ago, but they came by again with a whistle. Then I heard someone come in and I hid here. And you found me. You always find me, don't you, Mike?"

He nodded, forgetting that she couldn't see. But she felt his head move, and made a little sighing sound in the dark. "I guess you must have heard me coming in," he told her. "If you hadn't had the lid on so tight, you'd have heard me calling you."

"When can we leave?" she asked.

That jolted him back to the facts. The men must be almost up to this house by now. He wondered whether the cistern would save them, if the pirates really searched. "All for a silly piece of paper," he growled.

"But it might have saved us all, Mike. Really." She shivered in the coolness of the cistern. "Mike—is it so bad out there?"

"They're going to burn the town," he answered. She'd have to know the worst sooner or later. "There's at least one man who followed me in, and the rest may be here any minute."

"Oh, Mike. I'm sorry. I always make you

trouble, don't I?" Her voice was close to tears this time.

He made sh-h-h-ing sounds at her. There should be some noise from the pirates, if he could listen closely.

He heard nothing except the tantalizing drip of water from the walls below. He reached up cautiously, getting his back braced against a wall, and tried to lift the lid gently. It moved faintly, and a thin crack of light came through. There were sounds from outside, but too distant to be in the house. They sounded differ-

ent from the yells he had heard before, and farther up the street, though he couldn't be sure of that.

He lifted the lid farther, trying to place the sounds more exactly. Could the pirates have skipped this house? If they had, there might still be a chance!

The lid was higher now, and he turned his head to stick it out. His eyes froze.

Within six inches of his face stood a pair of legs!

He stopped breathing, but his mind was working now. The light was still faint, but it looked like the back of the legs. He tried not to move the lid as he turned his eyes in search of other legs, and found none. His right hand moved cautiously toward his pistol, found it, and brought it up.

It struck faintly against the lip of the cistern. The legs turned in a blur of movement, and the lid was suddenly ripped from Mike's hands.

"Stop or I shoot!" the boy ordered.

"Mike Boronda!" The voice was husky and weak, but it sounded familiar. "Thought I saw you come here."

Mike was still scared and suspicious. "Who are you?"

"Hawkins. Room enough for me?"

Mike almost fell off the timbers. He stood up, staring at the ugly, hairless face of the man who should have been a ghost—and almost looked like one. Hawkins laughed weakly, and let the lid sink to the floor. His long legs seemed uncertain as he crawled into the cistern beside Mike.

"Cover it," he muttered apologetically. "Yanking it up took the last bit of my strength."

Mike found the lid and moved it back into place. The pirates' voices were getting nearer again. "No chance for escape?"

"None!" Hawkins was breathing with difficulty in the tight space. "How'd you get here?"

Mike retold the story as quickly as he could, letting Hawkins fill in with his imagination. It was only after he finished that he remembered to introduce Maria. The boy was holding one ear close to the lip of the cistern, trying to listen for sounds from the pirates, and his voice was only a whisper. "And you?" he finished.

"I rowed. Others drowned before I could reach them. Caught fish with a piece of wire and a string I found. I ate them raw and I squeezed out their juices and drank that—sweet, like water, not salty. Native trick I learned. Hit the bay two nights ago. I couldn't navigate it with a compass, but I hit it by luck. Saw Bouchard's ships, but I couldn't have gone another mile. Slipped past in the dark, landed. I've been trying to find food and water most of the time, and a chance to get out of here. When I thought I recognized you out there, I came after you, but they saw me. Quite a chase before I shook them off and circled back. Then I thought I'd missed the house or you'd gone. I'm the reason they're so busy around here, I guess."

Mike shook his head in the dark, both at the speech and the facts. It was the longest speech he had ever heard Hawkins make, but he wished it might have been a lot longer. Only Hawkins could have done the impossible, but no one would ever know the full details.

Maria had been silent, trying to understand. She had learned English from Mike and his mother, but it was still imperfect. She tried to

speak to Hawkins, anyway. "You hongry, yes?"
At his grunt, she twisted on the timbers, and
Mike heard her fingers busy with something
that seemed to be tied beneath them. "Here,
you eat. Girl, she make big lunch. I don't eat
moch. Water in pail on rope here."

Hawkins grabbed the food in the dark, and
began shoving it into his mouth, not caring
what he was eating. Mike's mouth watered,
and his stomach seemed to flutter. He reached
over for the rope Maria had mentioned and
drew it up. There was at least a gallon of water
in the pail. He swallowed greedily and passed
it to Hawkins.

Hawkins passed it back, together with a
large piece of cooked beef. "You've been missing food too, Mike."

Even the sounds of feet entering the house
couldn't take all the pleasure of the food and
water from Mike then. He swallowed as silently as he could, while the feet moved about.
"Not here," a voice called out.

"He's got to be in one of these houses!"

"Sure, but what one? We ain't got all night.
We gotta get back to Corney and get the burning going."

The other voice considered it with a loud throat-clearing sound. "Burning? Look, we don't care if we find him or not—just so he ain't around. All we have to do is set fire to the whole set of houses here. We'll be burning 'em soon, anyhow. And then let him worry about hiding from that!"

Echoing sounds of admiration and laughter met the idea.

"Then let's start burning," the voice suggested.

A minute later the feet went stomping out toward the door. Mike lifted the cover and heard the sound of the pirate voices receding. But in its place was the warning crackle of fire.

Outside, the pirates were moving at the double from house to house, sometimes darting past a window with their torches held out in front. But Mike had no time now to worry about too much caution. He started to reach for the lid.

Hawkins was before him. The man must have regained a little strength. The lid slid off in his hands and he was out in the room. "More water," he ordered, and ran toward the flames that were spreading over the cheap bedding. His hands caught up a straw mat from the floor and beat it down on the flame. It was barely smoldering when Mike drew up the water and threw it over the bed.

The pirates were moving out now, before they could be caught in their own trap. Through the windows, Mike saw them rushing out of sight down the street, with every house near by already blazing. In a few minutes it would be impossible to get through the fire. The houses were close together here, and the shrubbery was dry enough to catch the fire and spread it.

"Your precious paper!" he growled at Maria.

She drew it from her clothes. "It *is* precious, Mike—it might stop the pirates from going on. See? A letter from Comandante de la Guerra to my uncle—you know, from Santa Barbara. He offers all possible help immediately."

"A fake—he'd have written to the Governor," Mike protested, trying to see it in the light of the fires. It looked genuine.

"No fake. Of course, it is a year old, and it was only an answer to my uncle's asking for some money. Uncle José did some favor for de la Guerra once, and he needed the money very badly. But it doesn't say what kind of help. If the pirates see it . . ."

Mike couldn't see how it could reach them without being given to them directly—which would make them suspicious—but it might be used. *If* they could get out in time. The flames now surrounded them completely.

Hawkins and Mike exchanged glances and moved as if geared together. Mike drew more water from the cistern, while Hawkins stripped the bed of all that would help them. They wetted the bedclothes thoroughly. Finally Hawkins poured water over all of them, after wrapping the letter in part of a piece of buckskin from a wall-drape.

The fire was worse, and growing hot enough to be felt inside the house. They wrapped the wet bedding about themselves as thickly as they could without making it impossible to run. For a moment they stood in the doorway, trying to find the best way of escape. Hawkins pointed. He and Mike each caught one of Maria's hands.

Their lungs were full of hot gases before they had been running ten seconds. Through the slits he had left in his blanket wrapping, Mike could see the fire ahead, and it seemed to be without end. He caught his breath, and tried to run faster. The damp clothes were steaming. Heat poured at him, running down his lungs, and licking up his legs.

Suddenly they were through it. The air was still hot, but there were no flames. They tore the bedding off themselves, and began to beat at the few flames that were licking at the damp clothes they wore. Most of them were from bits of wood that had clung to them.

All had burns, but they had been lucky, and none were too serious. Some of Maria's hair was charred. She moaned at the discovery, and then smiled ruefully. Lost hair was better than lost skin.

"That way," Mike suggested, pointing. "Maybe we can avoid the pirates, if we watch where the flames are."

Hawkins shook his head, flicking his eyes down at the bundle he had made of the letter, making sure it had come through the flames safely. "Will Corney be with them?"

Mike hesitated. "I suppose so. He's probably directing them from the center of it all."

"That way?" Hawkins waited for Mike's nod and started in the direction that might lead to Corney. The man bent beside Maria, repeating instructions until she nodded her understanding. After that, he turned to Mike.

"Corney wants you bad enough to chase you. Let him see you, try to keep the others from it. Wait until you can let him catch you. Tell him you're looking for him, want to sell him information. Then give him this. Or act scared, and try to hide it so he'll see it—whatever seems best—I'll need your pistol too!"

Mike nodded, took the letter, and handed the little gun to Hawkins. Well, he'd been willing to risk being captured to find Maria; he'd have to risk it now for all the others. He wondered what Hawkins' scheme was. Maybe it would work better if he did not know, though. Hawkins was a man who usually knew what he was doing.

After half an hour of dodging pirates and threading their way through the maze of streets, they didn't find Corney where they had expected. The town was apparently covered with pirates, all busy about some operation. Mike saw bladders of tallow being carried by one group; probably they were spreading it through the buildings to start the fires going more strongly. If they could scare Corney off before he gave the order to fire the town . . .!

But their time was getting short. Mike began searching his mind for another likely spot for Corney, but a band of pirates came past their hiding place, carrying more tallow.

"They must be from Corney," he guessed, and headed toward the place from which they had come. His reasoning proved sound. They could hear yells of instruction before they saw the pirates.

Corney was at one side of a little square, sitting awkwardly on a horse. From time to time, groups of pirates would come up to him and leave quickly for new work. There were only a few men with him permanently.

The three began working their way through the safer streets to the other side of the square, being doubly cautious not to bump into any pirates. It proved easier than they had expected. The pirates were burning furniture to light Corney's headquarters, and the light helped to show them as they moved outward.

Hawkins and Maria melted from sight into

separate doorways, and Mike edged his head around the corner of the street, looking into the square. Corney was still there, but nearer a house farther down. Mike slipped back around several of the houses, until he could move safely nearer to the pirate. He heard Hawkins and Maria behind, but he did not stop to watch where they hid this time.

Now Corney was less than ten feet away. Mike waited for a chance to see him alone. Men came and went, and it seemed that luck was against him.

Even as he decided it was impossible, Corney suddenly turned and rode back toward him, while the other men moved away.

Mike could wait no longer. He whistled softly.

Corney turned, but it was in answer to a shout from across the square. He called out an order. One man of a group detached himself and came back beside Corney. Mike muttered unhappily, drawing deeper into the shadows.

Corney climbed down from the horse—he couldn't be said to dismount—and began rubbing himself tenderly. The man grinned, and led the horse away slowly.

Mike edged closer again.

"Mr. Corney." It was too soft, and he swallowed, trying to clear his throat. His heart was thudding against his ribs worse than it had during the battle. He gripped the letter in one hand and wiped sweat off the other against his thighs, and tried again.

"Mr. Corney. It's Mike."

The pirate jerked around. "Where are you? Come out!"

"I can't. Your men would kill me if they saw me."

"Then get where *I* can see you." Corney's voice wasn't smooth now. He changed it quickly to its old casualness. "I want to know it's you, lad. With my own two eyes."

Mike stepped out of the shadow.

CHAPTER 10

The Last of the Pirates

ORNEY'S hand slapped toward his pistol, and Mike felt the blood freeze in his face; he wanted to run. Instead, he stepped forward, waving the letter. Corney hesitated. His eyes were darting about for a hidden ambush, but there was curiosity in them too. He moved closer.

"You dirty little traitor. Run off on me, will you?"

"And run back to you, too, sir," Mike told him. "Could I help it if the Dons caught me when I'd just found a horse to carry me after the priest? Blame Jim-Jim for letting him get away!"

Corney snorted. "Jim-Jim got thirty lashes for it. As for the priest, we found his body yesterday, where he'd hidden to die of his wound. For a priest, he was almost a man, though—so it was a decent burial I wasted on him." He chuckled. "Anyhow, it kept the men happier that way. Now then, what were you doing with the Dons when Jim-Jim saw you? You weren't any captive, by what I heard."

Mike had managed to keep his face straight as he heard of Padre Serra's death. The young priest had given his life to help Mike and Maria. It hurt to think that one of his oldest friends had been buried with scant ceremony among pirates. But he was sure that God must have been very fond of the soul of Padre Serra.

"Of course I wasn't a captive," he told Corney. "With the Don clothes I had on and a pretty story about how you captured me off my poor father's ship, they thought I was one of them. You know my Spanish is good enough to fool them. I just stayed with them until I could slip off with news you needed. And a fine time I had sneaking in here without being shot by one of our own men."

Mike paused to see how it was going. Corney was doubtful, but still waiting. He began again: "That's all. But d'ye truly think an Irish Obanion would be fighting for a King and against a free country?"

For the first time, Corney relaxed. "Now there's a point, Mike. I confess I thought well of you and hated to think you'd do a thing like that. Come tell me what news you have."

Now it was Mike's turn to hesitate. "And have your men see me and shoot me before you see how much I've done for you? You'll have to come back here before I go out in public."

"Sassy young puppy!" Corney had been letting Mike slip slowly back to a turn in the crooked street. Now he grinned, and came forward, still holding the gun, but not aiming it directly at the boy. "But I like a lad with spirit—I'd begun to fear you lacked it. All right, let's have what you hold there."

"For my safety," Mike suggested.

"For safety, if it's good. And it had better be that, me lad."

They were just out of view of the square now, but still within easy shouting distance, if Corney wanted to yell for help. Mike knew he could go back no farther. He handed over the letter reluctantly, as if unsure of his wisdom.

Corney opened it with one hand, still holding the gun in the other. He moved back half a step toward the light and began scowling over it, straining his eyes to make the most of what he could see. His glance jumped to the letter and back to the street repeatedly, caution still strong in him.

Then he whistled. "Mike, me darlin', you bring bad news but news I'm glad to know of. How'd you steal it . . ."

The words chopped off. Hawkins had slipped out of the shadows across the street before even Mike had seen him. One hand yanked the letter from Corney's fingers while the pistol he had borrowed from Mike struck down at Corney's other wrist. The pirate's gun dropped to the ground.

"You weel be quiet," Hawkins stated coldly. "I do not like to make noise weez ze peestol, bot I do like to keel you."

Corney opened his mouth, then thought better of it. Hawkins had been motioning Mike behind Corney's back. The boy broke into a run, away from the light.

Hawkins caught Mike with a single bound, twisting in air until he still faced Corney with the pistol. He yanked Mike around in front of him, drew back his hand, and struck.

The blow had been judged exactly. It looked bad, but was hardly more than a push when it struck. Mike toppled to the ground and groaned as realistically as he could.

"Juan!" Hawkins called. Corney had been about to spring, or to yell. He was tensed for something. Now he halted.

A heavy stick struck the back of the pirate's skull before the man could do anything. He collapsed soundlessly.

Hawkins inspected him. "Good, Maria. He'll live. Had to use a bad accent—I can't speak Spanish. Now—out!"

They were none too soon. Someone was yelling for Corney in the square, and the sound of racing feet headed toward them. A faint groan came from the pirate's lips as they ducked around a corner.

It had been a good scheme, Mike thought. And there had probably been less risk than he had believed. Hawkins must have been close enough to protect him all the time.

He could think of no better way of delivering the false letter. Corney must think Mike had been sincere, but that the Spanish had followed him. "He probably figures I'm going to be strung up on a tree, now that you've captured me and the letter again," he told Hawkins.

"Maybe not." Hawkins was breathing hard,

as if the exertion had been almost too much
for his weakened body, but his voice held its
normal unemotional quality. "He can't take
chances."

It was true. Even if Corney thought it was
staged for his benefit, the pirates couldn't
afford to gamble. They had little to gain by
chasing down the Salinas after the ranchers if
there was any possibility that troops might be
moving to meet them.

Mike hadn't realized how much of the night
had passed. He looked up now, following
Hawkins' worried glance, to see light already
showing in the sky. He took Maria's hand, and
with Hawkins in the lead, they twisted and
turned their way through the streets. Watching for pirates made their escape tediously
slow.

They still had some distance to go to get out
of the town. And it would soon be too light for
safe travel. They hastened their steps, trying
more for speed than caution now. The pirates
were busy about something in the distance,
but there was no way of telling whether they
were planning to leave or simply to go ahead
with their burning.

"They'd have a few days for nastiness before troops could arrive," Hawkins muttered to Mike.

They would, the boy realized. And during those few days, if they decided to risk staying, they could terrorize the whole valley. Nothing was settled.

Then smoke began drifting out of one of the houses. There were no pirates about, but soon another bit of smoke drifted up, and another. They'd been planting fuses with the tallow, and had set them to go off about at the same time. Fuses from the fort, Mike thought—their own supplies used against them!

But the fire was catching quickly now, spreading in a way that showed a liberal use of the tallow. Ahead of them, flames were rising sharply. Hawkins scowled, and let Mike take the lead. He had no time for worrying about the future of the valley, now that they were in danger of being ringed in by flames.

Suddenly Hawkins caught Mike and drew him and Maria back into the shelter of a doorway. Jim-Jim had just turned the corner into the street they were on!

The pirate was armed with two guns and

assorted knives, and his speed was mixed with a measure of caution that indicated he was looking for something.

"Corney suspects," Hawkins guessed. "He's looking for us!"

Knowing who it was, Mike was even more sure of it, though it might have been Jim-Jim's own idea to try to trail him.

There was no chance to escape, and the rising flames would soon make it impossible to hide here. Anyhow, the buildings here had been stripped completely, and even their hide doors had been slashed down. It was a good street to take them out of the city quickly, but the worst in which to stay.

Hawkins pushed Mike and Maria back against a far corner and flattened himself against a doorway. His ears seemed to take on a life of their own. He waited, without a sound. Jim-Jim's steps came closer.

When Mike was just about ready to scream with the tension, Hawkins grinned awkwardly. He still waited, though. Then he stepped out quietly.

There was a strangled grunt, and Mike rushed out just in time to see the big Sandwich

Islander pitch end-over-end and land on the
base of his neck.

"Dead," Hawkins told them. "Dead before
I let go. Wait." He leaned against the wall with
legs that shook, catching his breath in ragged
gasps. His hollow eyes were on the pirate mate,
and he pointed. "Bottle."

Mike pulled out the bottle and handed it to
Hawkins, who took one brief pull at it and
threw it away.

"Sometimes a little helps," the man said.

His breathing was easier, and he straightened up. "Medicine. I'm all right—just can't do too much too fast. Let's go."

They had to hurry. Five minutes later they were near the last of the buildings at the edge of town, and the road to the Robles ranch lay directly before them.

The light was still dim enough to make shooting difficult, and it might help them to escape without being seen. Hawkins and Mike conferred quickly, picking out a route. At Mike's nod, they broke into a run. Hawkins must have drawn his strength from some miraculous source, because he kept up with them until they dropped into a shallow arroyo. They rested a moment, and rushed forward again.

The third dash brought them to a clump of oak that would be their last stop. From there on, they'd be out of rifle range. Mike crashed through the trees toward a larger arroyo he knew was on the other side. He went over the edge of the bank without looking.

Hands caught him in mid-stride.

His heart missed a beat. Then it settled back to normal; the hands belonged to Feliciano Soberanes! There were ten soldiers waiting with him. One of them was lying on the ground, though; Hawkins rubbed his knuckles and bent forward to help the man up.

"Mistake," the mate said ruefully.

Estrada was hugging Maria as Soberanes explained that they had been waiting on the faint chance that Mike or the girl might try to escape. The officer would not let any of the men follow into the town, but it was worth a chance of waiting here for them in case they needed help. They'd just been leaving when the fire had caught their attention.

It was growing light now. Soberanes lifted Mike onto his horse, Estrada took Maria, and Hawkins swung onto the extra horse that they had brought. Mike wasn't surprised to see that the mate rode as if born in the saddle. They moved off at an easy canter, while Mike told the important part of the story.

When he was finished, Soberanes rode toward the girl. His hat swept from his head and he bowed. "A foolish girl you are, Maria Estrada, but a very brave and good one." He held his hand out to Hawkins silently, sensing that it was the finest way of showing his thanks to the taciturn mate.

But it was to Mike that he paid the highest compliment. His arms lifted slightly, depositing the reins of his big gray stallion in Mike's hands, while his own dropped to his side.

Now they turned by common consent and looked back at the town. It rivaled the dawn light, with flames shooting up into the air. Even at this distance, a steady crackle and roar seemed to come from it. Beside the fort, the pirates were drawn up with their booty, apparently watching.

No spot in the town had escaped. Houses, public buildings, shrubbery—all were burning brightly. Even the streets seemed aflame.

Estrada turned to the land with its rolling hills and ever blooming flowers. "Beautiful, like life in Monterey could be. But is it a land for soldiers? There is no city. What will become of us now? The missions are doomed; the King will surely crush them. Our homes are in flames. There is nothing here for us but beauty, and we cannot live on that."

It had come, Mike realized. Even without pirate raids into the valley, men of the high ability and courage of Estrada could take no more.

But Soberanes was looking across the country too. "Beautiful, and fruitful. My father once held the Buena Vista Ranch before it reverted to the missions. Now that the missions are going, we can petition for it back. The Governor may be weak, but he'll be grateful—if the pirates leave! I have always thought the future lies with the land. And there's enough for every grown man among us to have a grant of at least fifteen thousand acres."

"And I have four sons already grown." Estrada looked up, only half-believing. Then his face sobered. "The Governor could not refuse a faithful soldier, true. But what good will it do when the taxes of the King take all the profits and we can have nothing to do with other trading countries?"

They rode on in silence, each staring back at the flaming ruins of their home city, and wondering what the pirates would do. If they were to be killed fighting a raid into the valley, the future wouldn't matter!

Estrada picked it up again. "Yet Mexico tried to free herself from Spain, and I hear she will try again, like Argentina, but with no

pirates to help. Argentina has shown it can be
done. Then trade would come. If . . ."

"The King is far away—so far he cannot see
our need for help or soldiers, and has left us
to this." Soberanes pointed back to the city.
"Maybe he is also too far to hold us."

Mike nodded. The pirates had proved that

Monterey could never depend on a rule from six thousand miles away. This could be a great country—perhaps even as powerful as the United States felt it would be.

If . . . It was always true only if the pirates left.

They reached the camp at last, and Mike let out a sudden cry and dropped from the saddle. He rushed forward, to be caught up in the rough, strong arms of his uncle. Behind his uncle's firm, smiling face, the voice of his mother sounded, crying his name.

She was walking, though a little uncertainly, and she still looked weak. Mike dropped to his knees and buried his head in her dress, crying and not ashamed of it, while his uncle patted his head with his left hand. The right was busy wringing that of Hawkins.

It was half an hour later when a shout startled them all and brought them to the side of Soberanes.

Already Monterey was a wreck, its buildings gutted. Soberanes was not watching that. He was pointing to boats that were putting out from the shore toward the *Argentina* and the *Santa Rosa*. They were full boats, low in the water. Some of the load might have been loot, but most of it was a burden of close-packed men.

The trick had worked. The pirates were taking no chances.

Nobody cheered. Too much damage had been done for cheering to be possible. But they stood silently, watching the boats carry the men aboard the ships. Finally, the last boat rose up on its grapnels. They could see the big anchor coming up to its resting place on the *Argentina,* and both ships were raising sail.

There was a fresh breeze, and the sails bellied out. The two ships slid from the harbor, gathering speed slowly. They began turning south beyond Point Piños, heading toward South America, where Argentina would discover to her regret the type of beasts she had recruited to help her fight for God and Country.

"Perhaps they won," Soberanes said, breaking the long silence. "Perhaps because houses are ruined, we will creep back to Mexico. But I think they have perhaps left us something— the knowledge that men who would be more than slaves must be their own protectors."

Below, the charred mass of ruins looked up at them. The work of fifty years had been wiped out, and most of the people around Soberanes were homeless. But there was none of the bitterness Mike had expected. A faint cheer went up as Soberanes finished.

Maria turned her face toward Mike, and he saw the people smile. He looked toward Soberanes.

"Do you think I could petition for a land grant when I'm older?" he asked.

Soberanes laughed suddenly. "No, not when you're older, Miguel. You're a soldier and a man now, and you'll petition for your land when I do. Will you like that?"

"We'll like that," Mike told him. Maria nodded.

They looked across the sweeping hills to the harbor, and back to the country around them. Once this had been Monterey—and some day it would be Monterey again.

But it was always home.